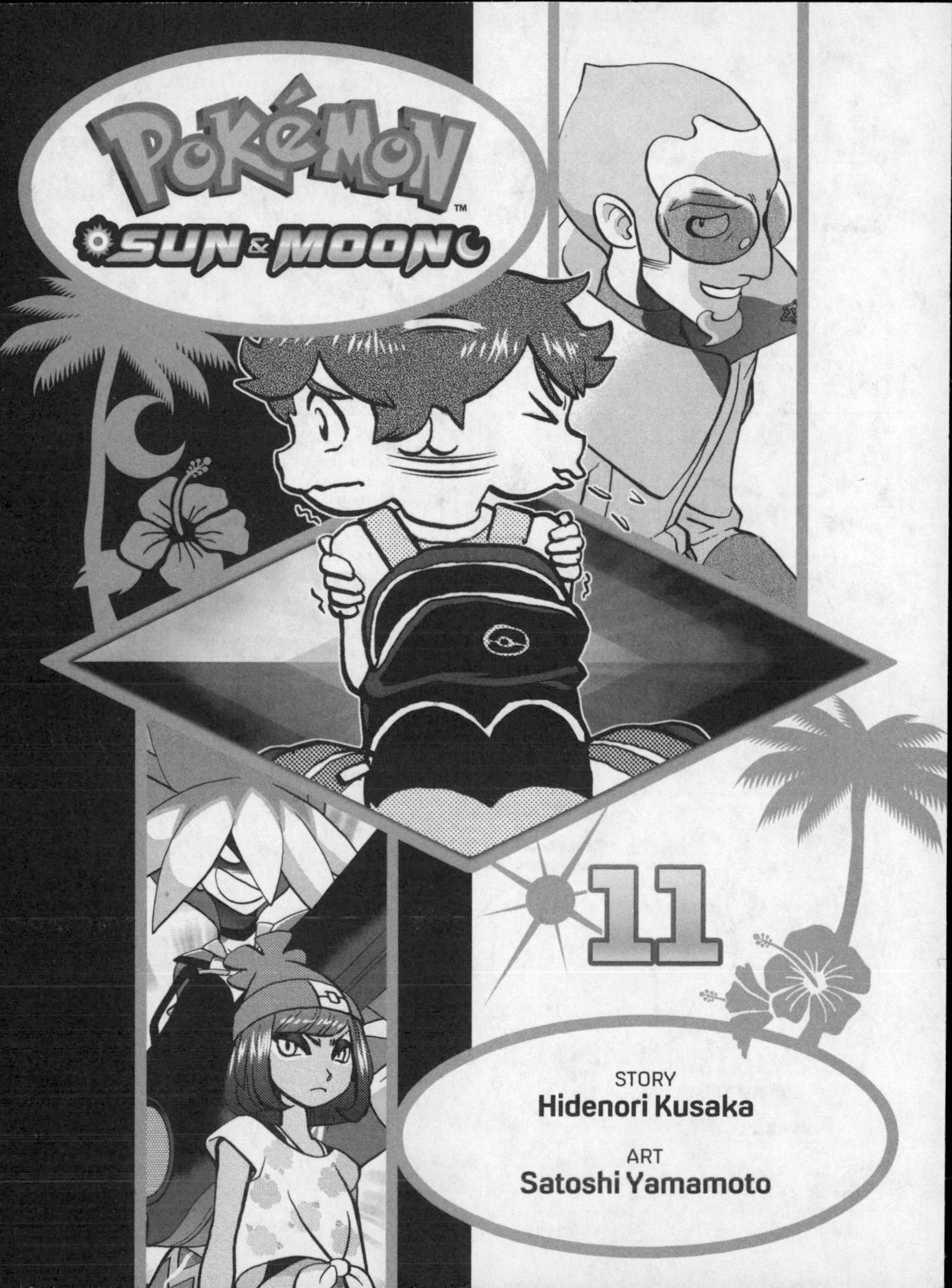

Pokémon™ Sun & Moon

11

STORY
Hidenori Kusaka

ART
Satoshi Yamamoto

Introduction

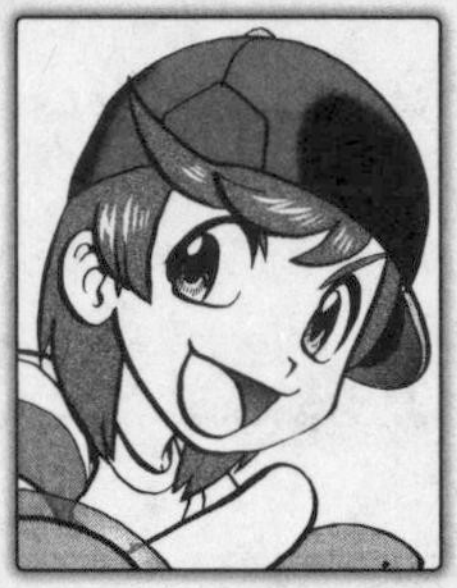

Sun

He was dragged into the Aether Foundation's scheme and disappeared into Ultra Space. It took him six months to escape.

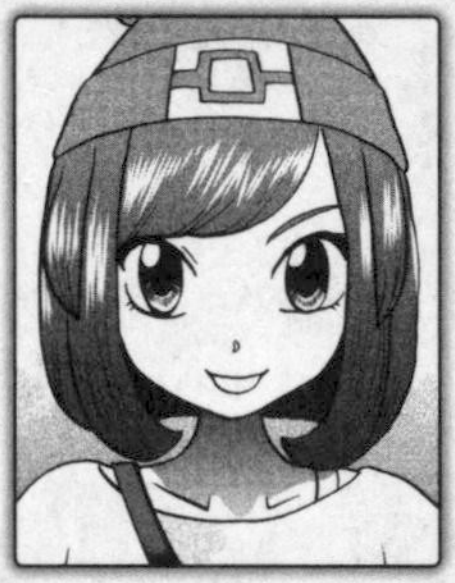

Moon

A pharmacist who has traveled to Alola from a faraway region. She is a self-confident original thinker and an excellent archer.

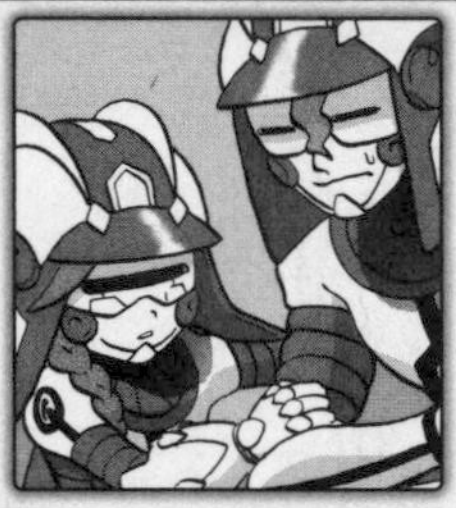

Ultra Recon Squad

Mysterious people from another dimension who travel to Alola to conduct some sort of investigation.

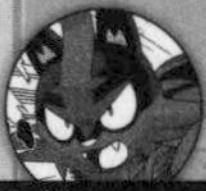

Dollar (Torracat)

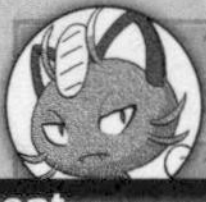

Cent (Alolan Meowth)

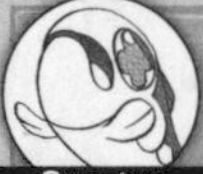

Quarter (Wishiwashi)

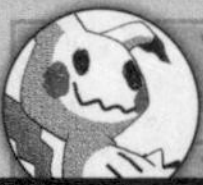

Penny (Mimikyu)

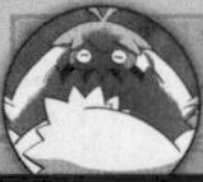

Loot (Crabominable)

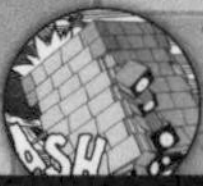
SH

Ray (Stakataka)

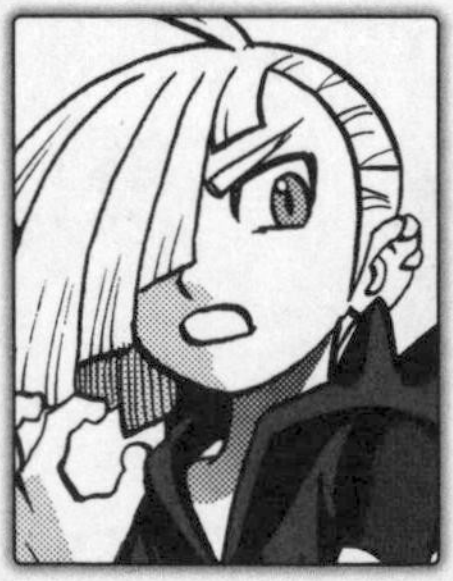

Gladion

Lillie's brother. His partner is Silvally, a man-made Pokémon created specifically to fight against the Ultra Beasts!

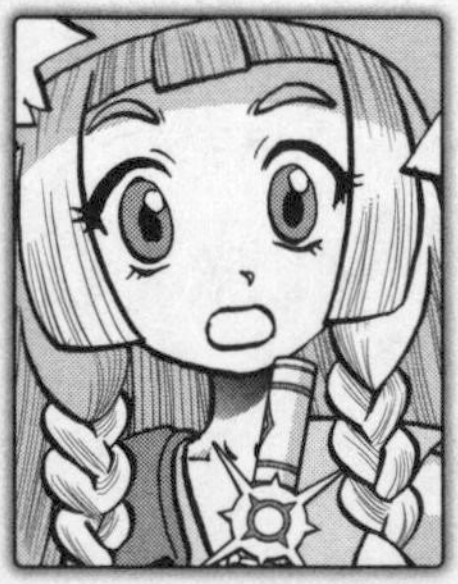

Lillie

Lusamine's daughter and Gladion's timid younger sister. She has recently learned the importance of depending on other people.

Character

Guzma

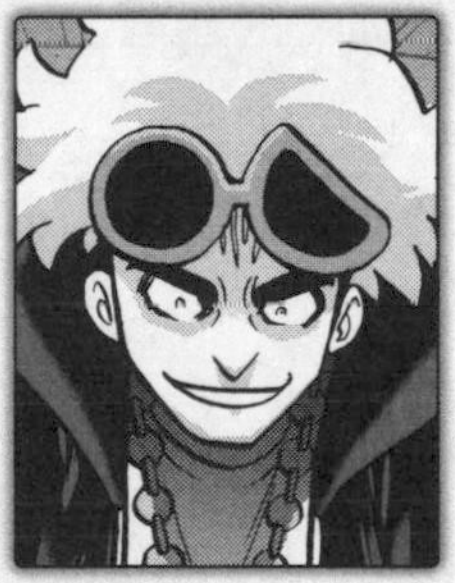

The leader of Team Skull. He was taken away by Nihilego and went missing, but he managed to escape to Poni Island.

Lusamine

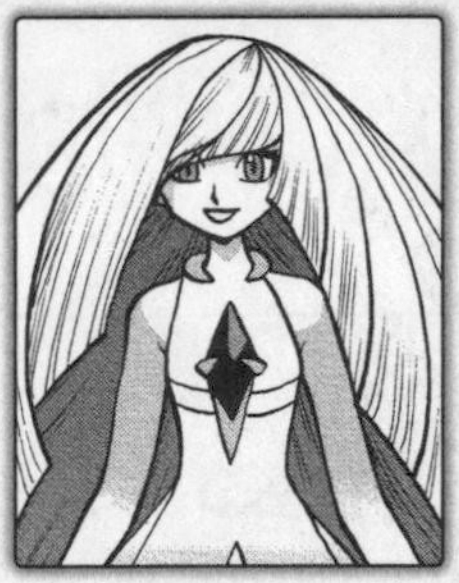

The president of the Aether Foundation who is obsessed with the Ultra Beasts. She is Gladion and Lillie's mother. She seems to have succeeded in creating a paradise for the Ultra Beasts, but...?!

Faba

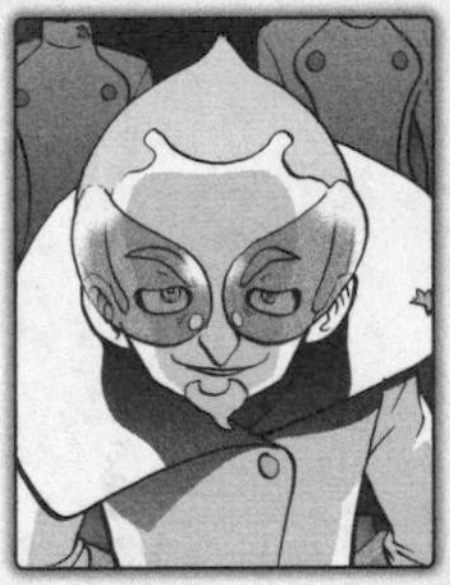

The self-centered and ambitious branch chief of the Aether Foundation. Long ago, he stole the island that belonged to Sun's great-grandfather.

The Story Thus Far...

Moon, a pharmacist from another region, comes to the flower-filled vacation paradise of the Alola region, which consists of numerous tropical islands. While on an important errand, Moon meets Sun, who works various odd jobs and runs a delivery service to reach his goal of saving up a million dollars. When the Island Guardians of the Alolan Islands, called Tapu, become agitated, Sun is chosen to complete the island challenge to soothe the Tapus' anger. Moon comes along to help. Sun successfully completes the challenge by delivering a special Berry to the Tapu on different islands. While on the island of Poni, Sun and Moon play the legendary Sun and Moon flutes, causing two Cosmoem to transform into Solgaleo, the emissary of the sun, and Lunala, the emissary of the moon! Sun and Moon are sucked into the crack in the sky and find themselves in a mysterious world called the Ultra Space, where they meet Lusamine, president of the Aether Foundation, who has been possessed by Nihilego! Moon tries to free Lusamine by capturing Nihilego! She shoots an arrow toward Lusamine as a bright light illuminates the sky.

CONTENTS

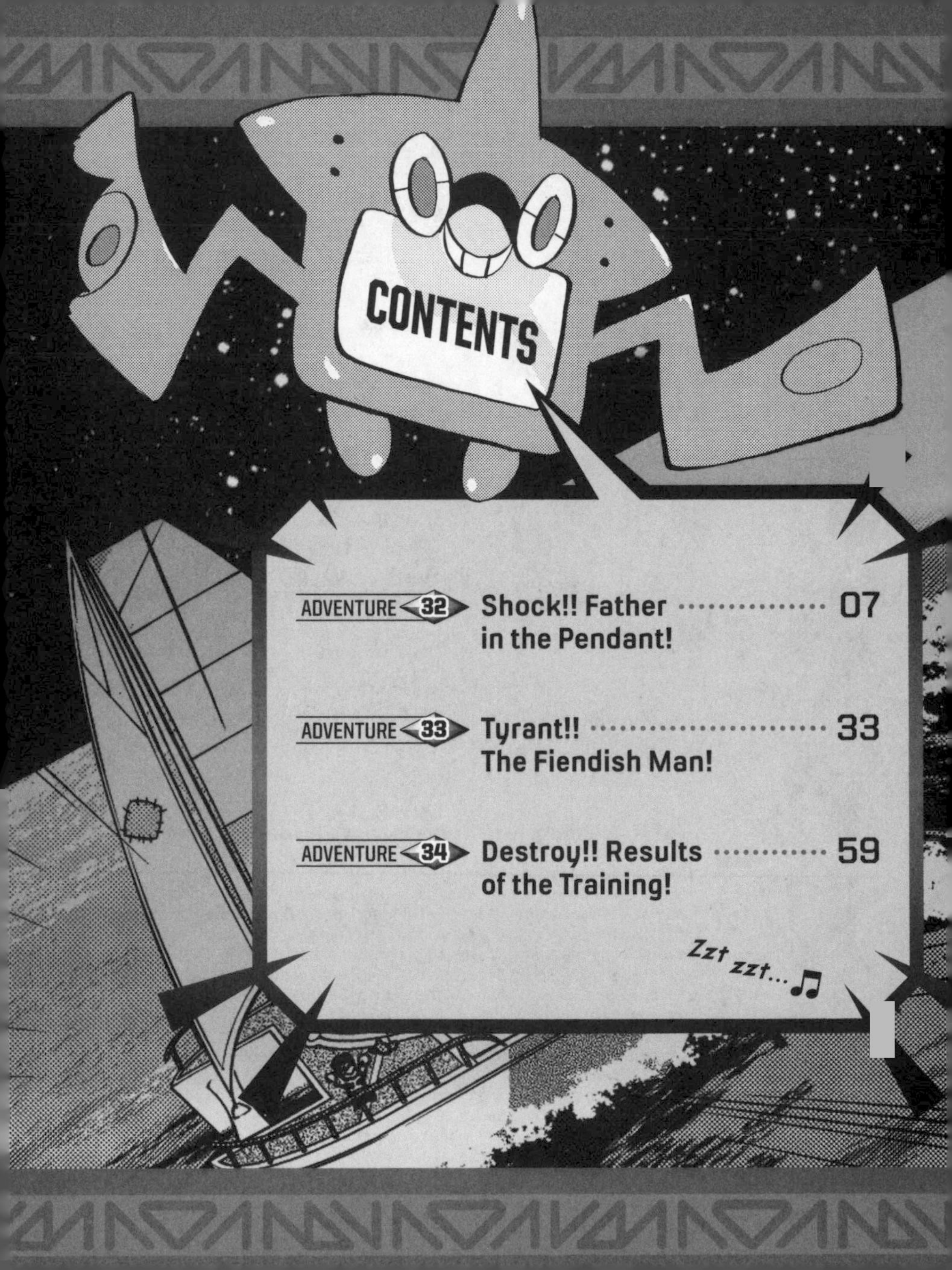
Zzt zzt...♫

Adventure 32
Shock!! Father in the Pendant!

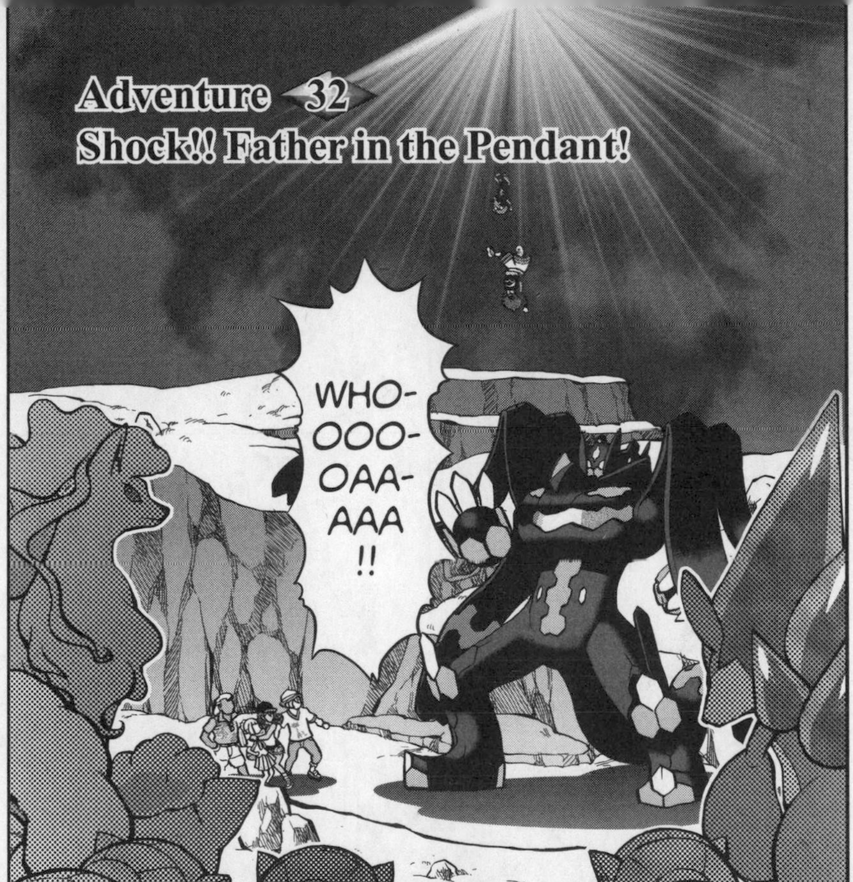
WHO-
OOO-
OAA-
AAA
!!

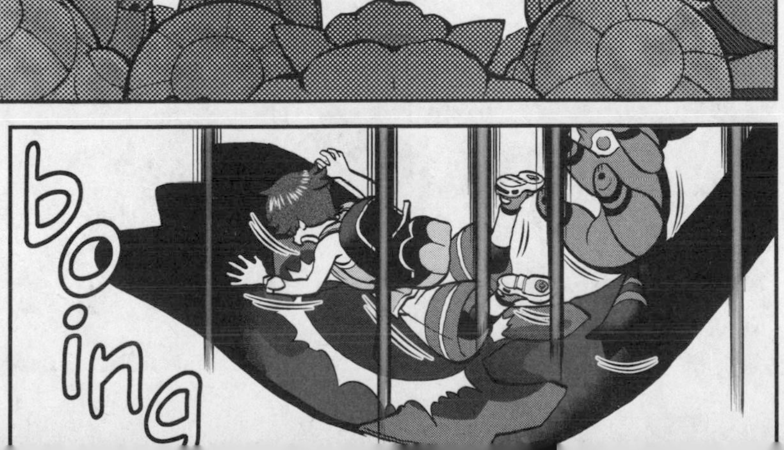
boing

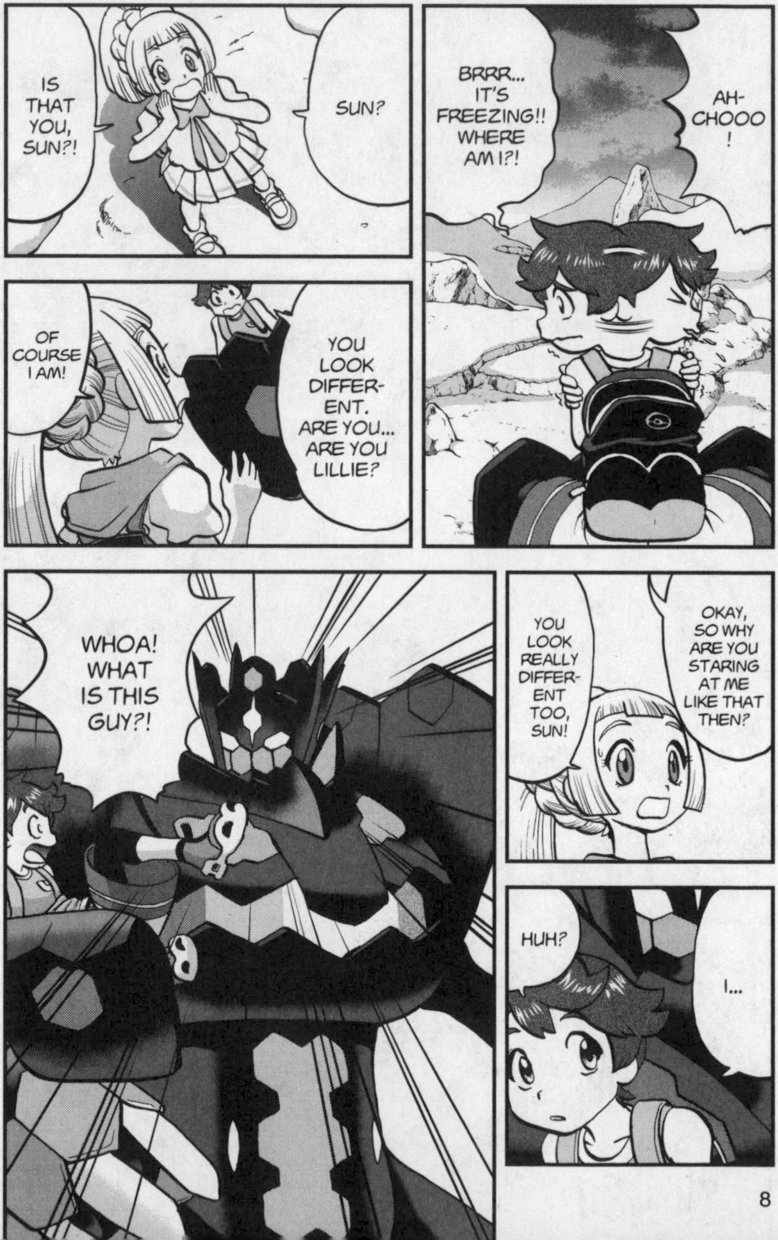
AH-CHOOO!
BRRR... IT'S FREEZING!! WHERE AM I?!
SUN?
IS THAT YOU, SUN?!
YOU LOOK DIFFER-ENT. ARE YOU... ARE YOU LILLIE?
OF COURSE I AM!
OKAY, SO WHY ARE YOU STARING AT ME LIKE THAT THEN?
YOU LOOK REALLY DIFFER-ENT TOO, SUN!
I...
HUH?
WHOA! WHAT IS THIS GUY?!

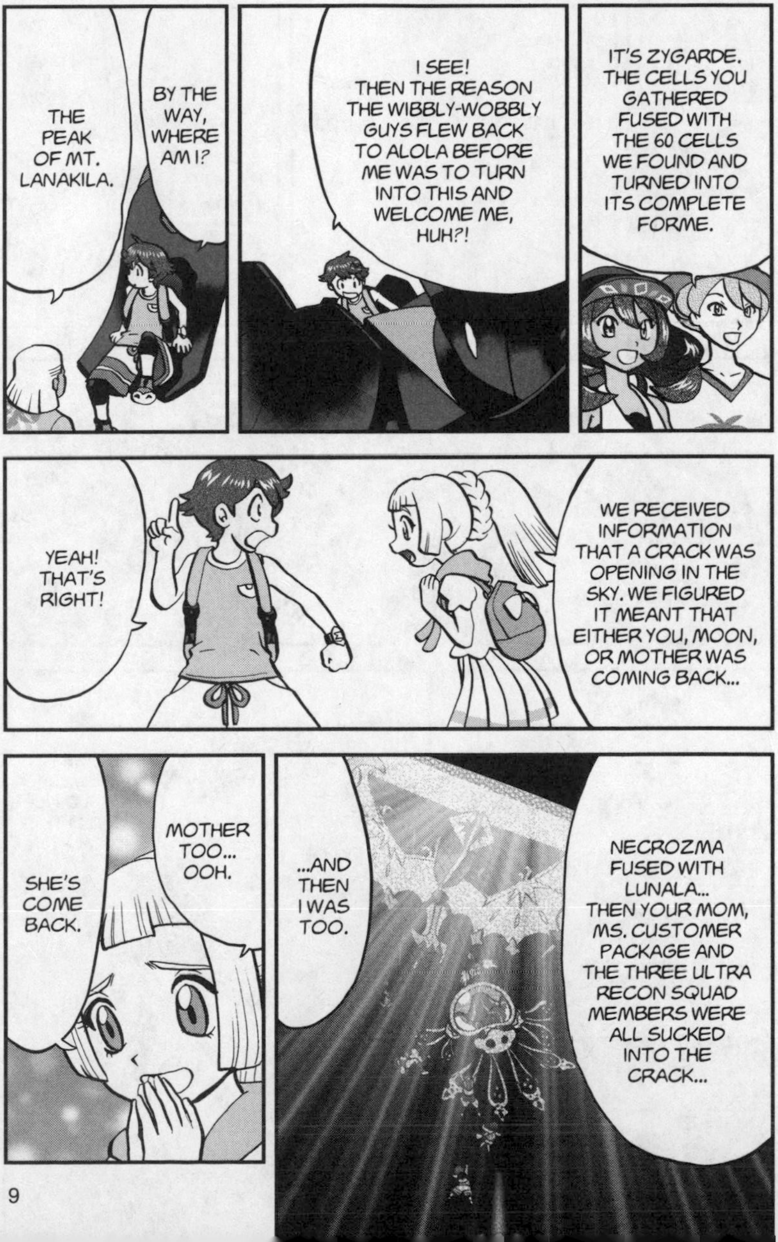
IT'S ZYGARDE. THE CELLS YOU GATHERED FUSED WITH THE 60 CELLS WE FOUND AND TURNED INTO ITS COMPLETE FORME.
I SEE! THEN THE REASON THE WIBBLY-WOBBLY GUYS FLEW BACK TO ALOLA BEFORE ME WAS TO TURN INTO THIS AND WELCOME ME, HUH?!
BY THE WAY, WHERE AM I?
THE PEAK OF MT. LANAKILA.
WE RECEIVED INFORMATION THAT A CRACK WAS OPENING IN THE SKY. WE FIGURED IT MEANT THAT EITHER YOU, MOON, OR MOTHER WAS COMING BACK...
YEAH! THAT'S RIGHT!
NECROZMA FUSED WITH LUNALA... THEN YOUR MOM, MS. CUSTOMER PACKAGE AND THE THREE ULTRA RECON SQUAD MEMBERS WERE ALL SUCKED INTO THE CRACK...
...AND THEN I WAS TOO.
MOTHER TOO... OOH.
SHE'S COME BACK.

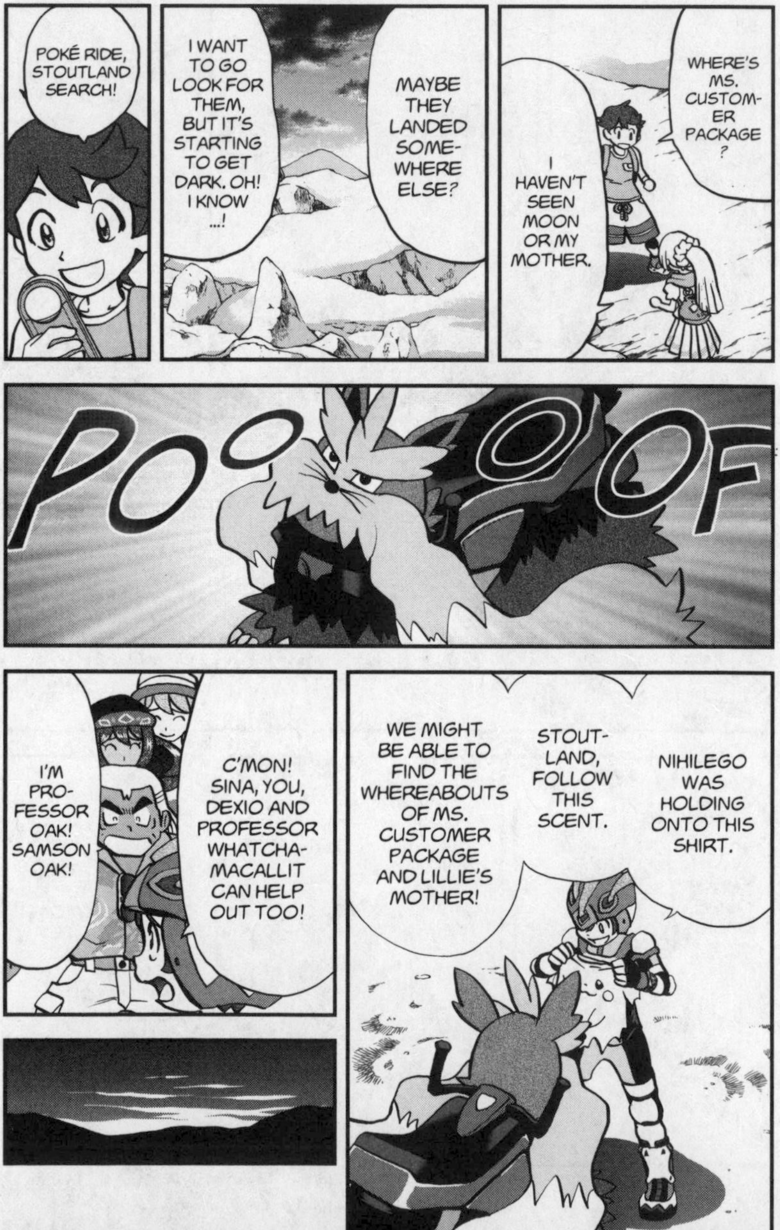
WHERE'S MS. CUSTOMER PACKAGE?
I HAVEN'T SEEN MOON OR MY MOTHER.
MAYBE THEY LANDED SOMEWHERE ELSE?
I WANT TO GO LOOK FOR THEM, BUT IT'S STARTING TO GET DARK. OH! I KNOW...!
POKÉ RIDE, STOUTLAND SEARCH!
POOOOF
NIHILEGO WAS HOLDING ONTO THIS SHIRT.
STOUTLAND, FOLLOW THIS SCENT.
WE MIGHT BE ABLE TO FIND THE WHEREABOUTS OF MS. CUSTOMER PACKAGE AND LILLIE'S MOTHER!
C'MON! SINA, YOU, DEXIO AND PROFESSOR WHATCHAMACALLIT CAN HELP OUT TOO!
I'M PROFESSOR OAK! SAMSON OAK!

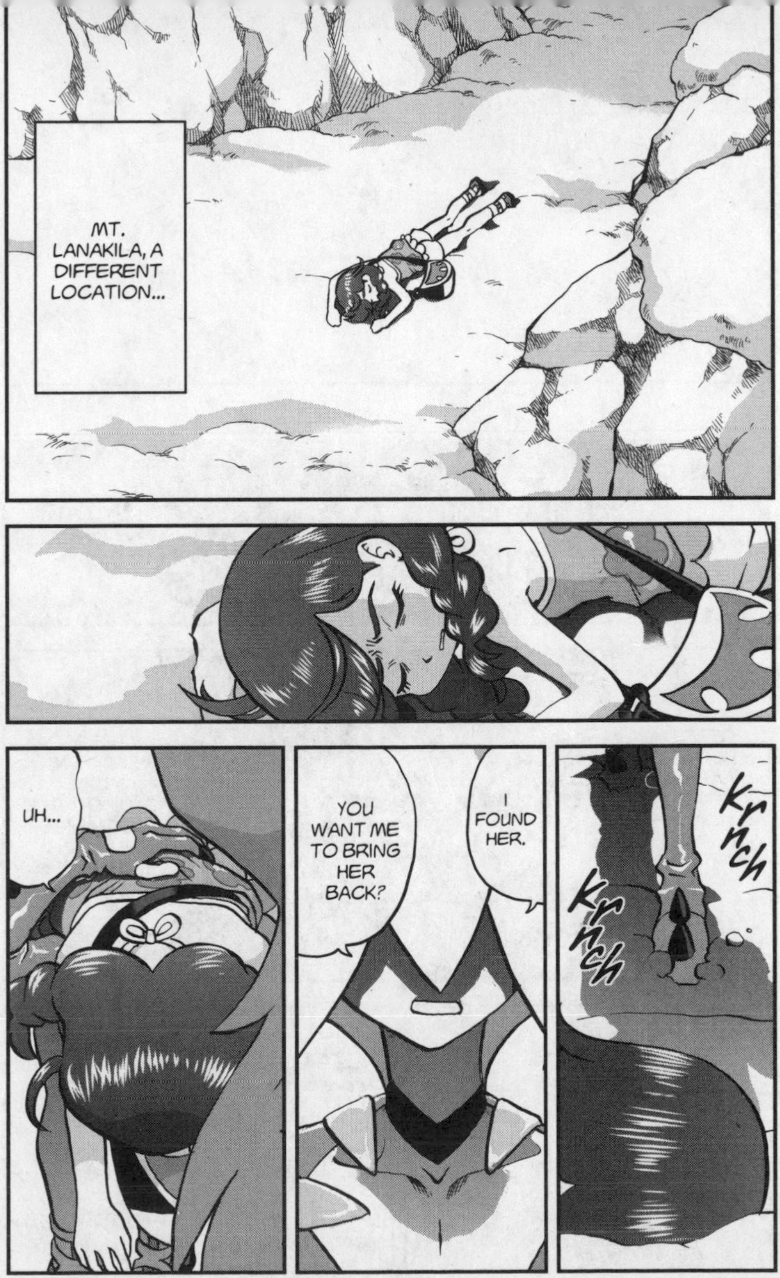
MT. LANAKILA, A DIFFERENT LOCATION...
Krnch
Krnch
I FOUND HER.
YOU WANT ME TO BRING HER BACK?
UH...

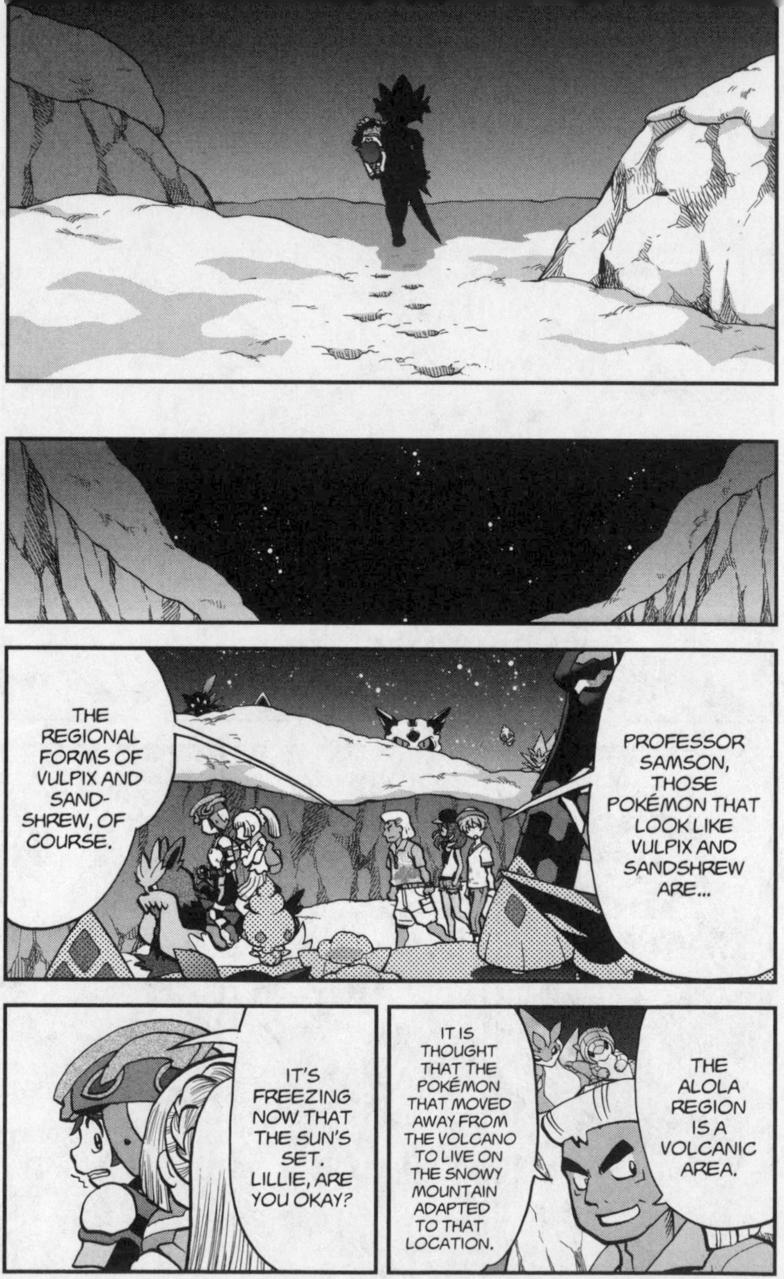
PROFESSOR SAMSON, THOSE POKÉMON THAT LOOK LIKE VULPIX AND SANDSHREW ARE...
THE REGIONAL FORMS OF VULPIX AND SAND-SHREW, OF COURSE.
THE ALOLA REGION IS A VOLCANIC AREA.
IT IS THOUGHT THAT THE POKÉMON THAT MOVED AWAY FROM THE VOLCANO TO LIVE ON THE SNOWY MOUNTAIN ADAPTED TO THAT LOCATION.
IT'S FREEZING NOW THAT THE SUN'S SET. LILLIE, ARE YOU OKAY?

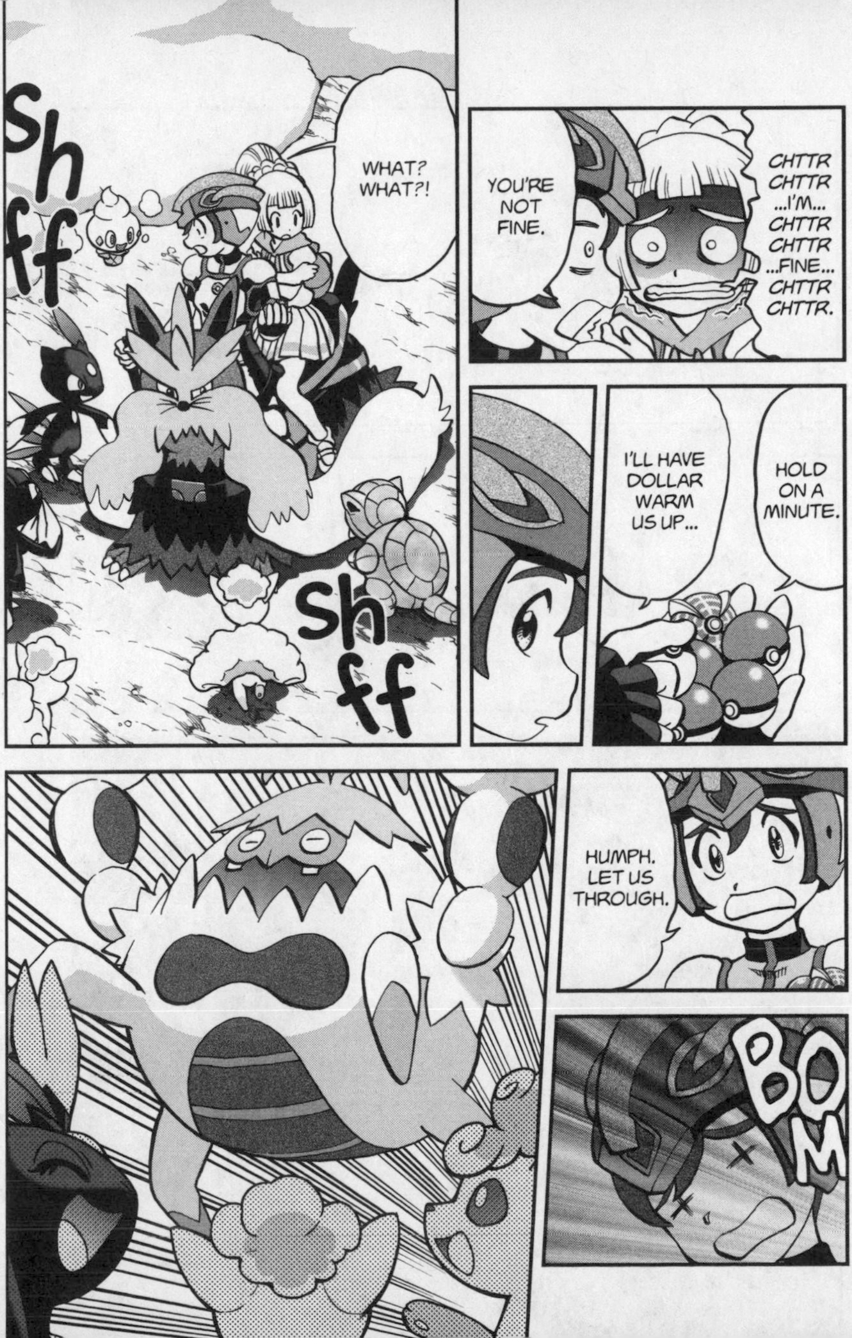
CHTTR CHTTR ...I'M... CHTTR CHTTR ...FINE... CHTTR CHTTR.
YOU'RE NOT FINE.
HOLD ON A MINUTE.
I'LL HAVE DOLLAR WARM US UP...
WHAT? WHAT?!
Shff
Shff
HUMPH. LET US THROUGH.
BOOM

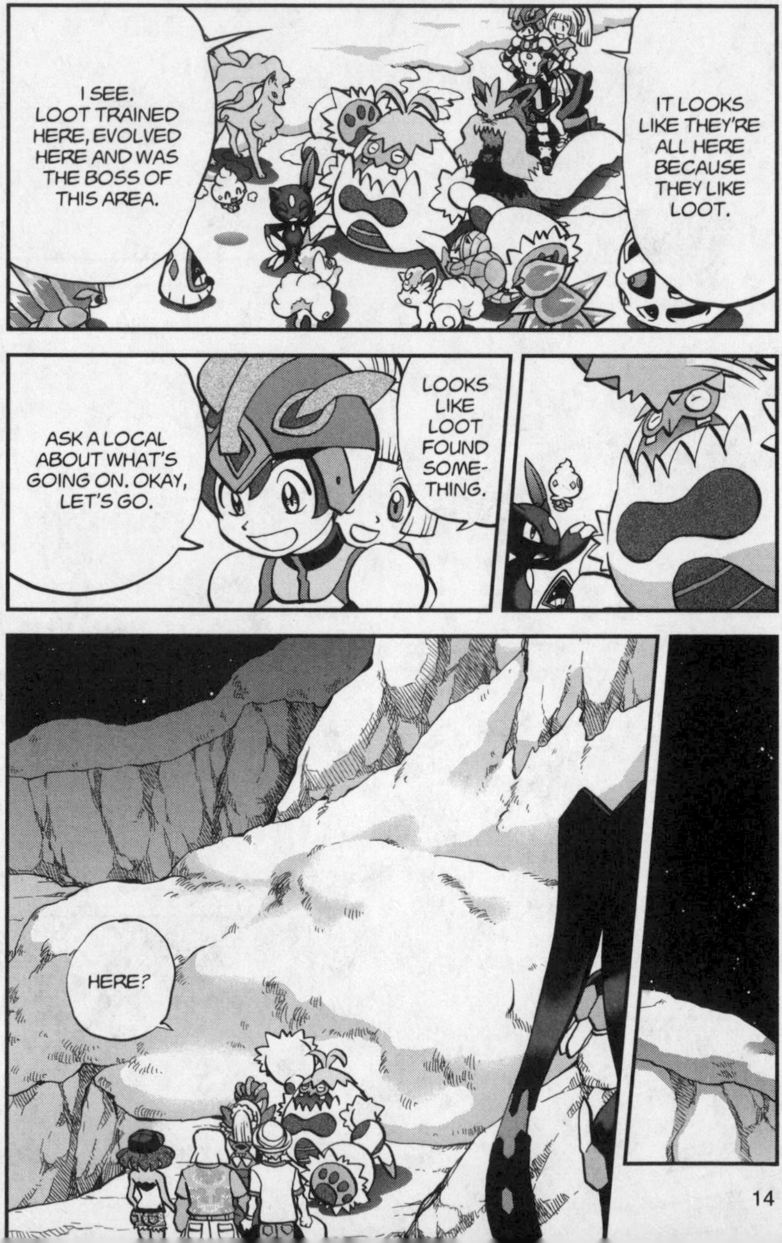
IT LOOKS LIKE THEY'RE ALL HERE BECAUSE THEY LIKE LOOT.
I SEE. LOOT TRAINED HERE, EVOLVED HERE AND WAS THE BOSS OF THIS AREA.
LOOKS LIKE LOOT FOUND SOME-THING.
ASK A LOCAL ABOUT WHAT'S GOING ON. OKAY, LET'S GO.
HERE?

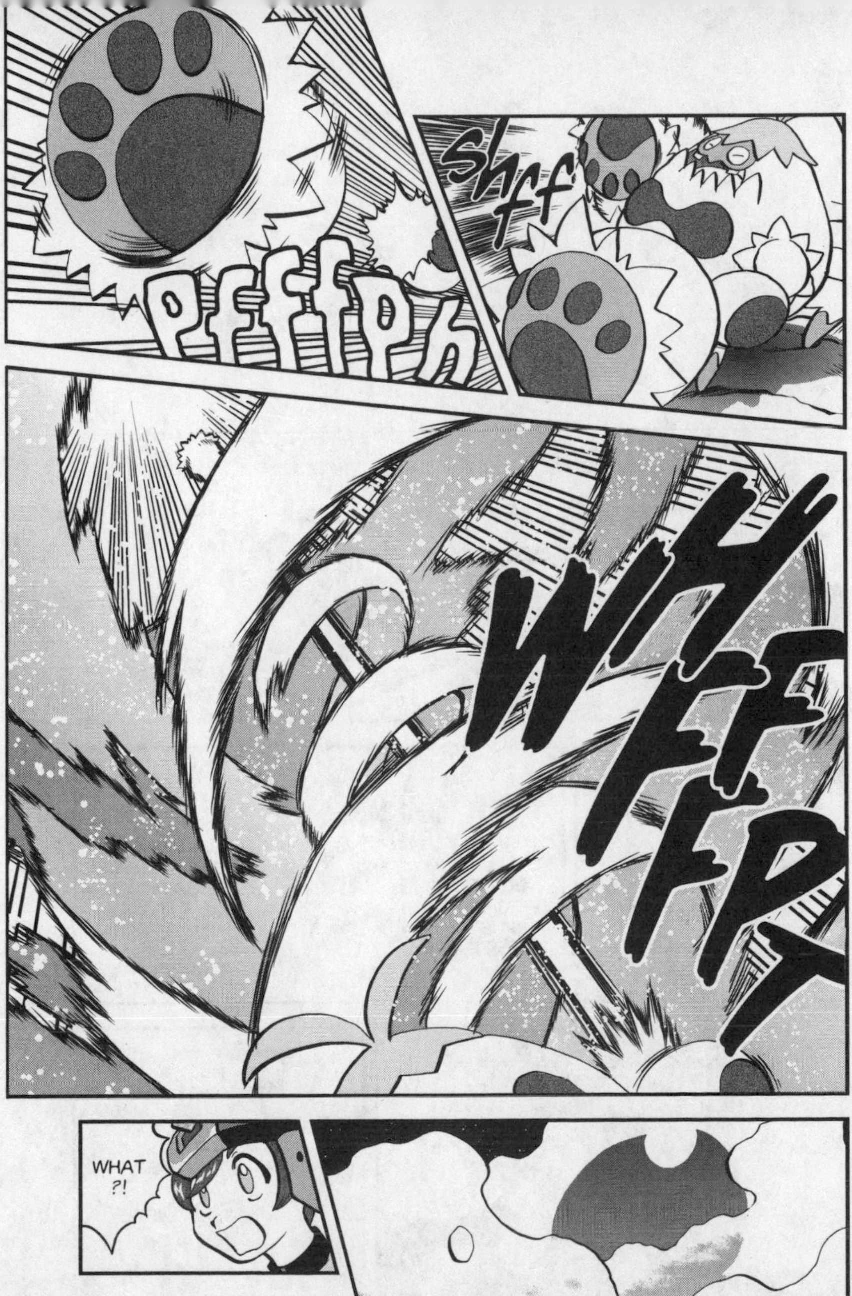
shff
pfffph
WHFFP
WHAT ?!

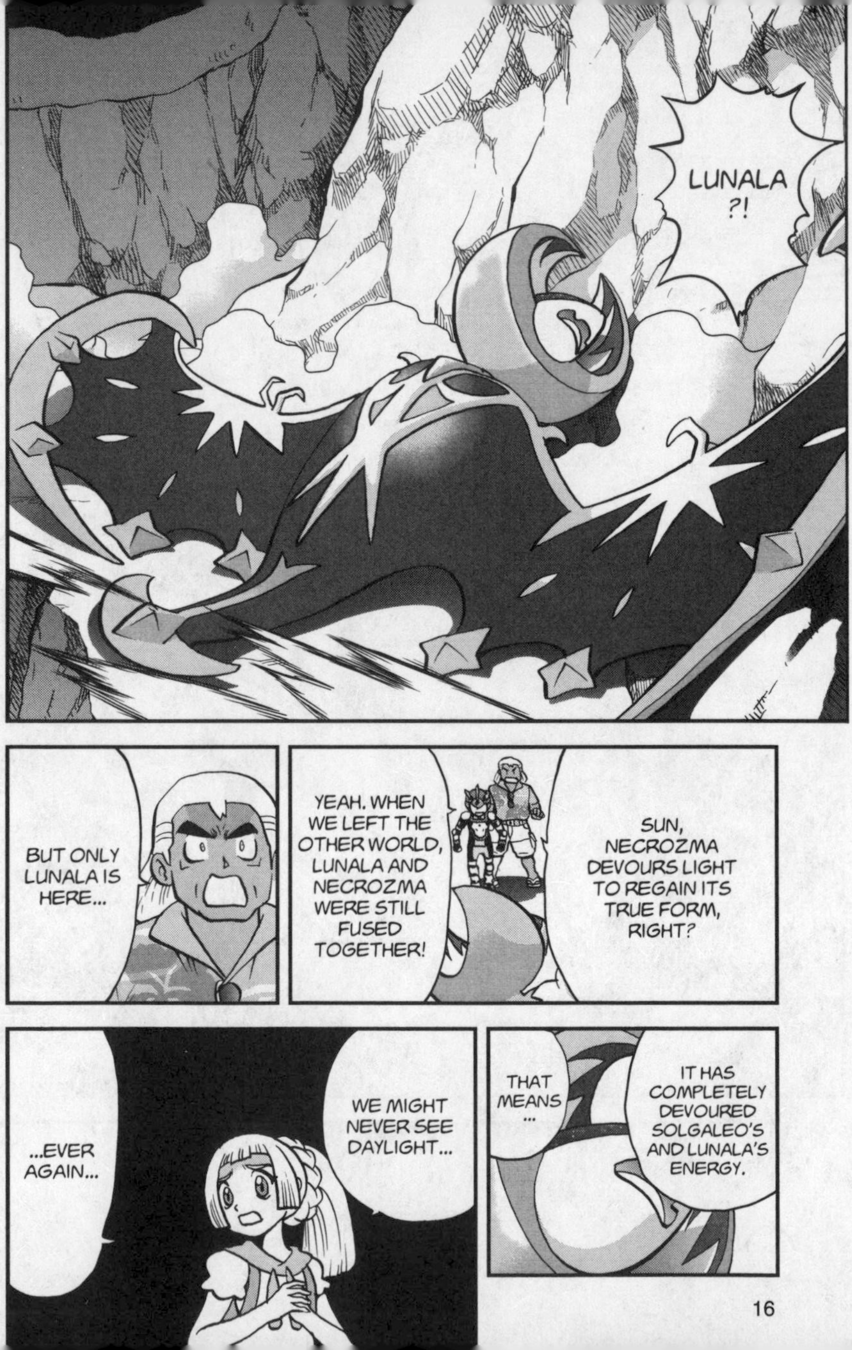
LUNALA ?!
SUN, NECROZMA DEVOURS LIGHT TO REGAIN ITS TRUE FORM, RIGHT?
YEAH. WHEN WE LEFT THE OTHER WORLD, LUNALA AND NECROZMA WERE STILL FUSED TOGETHER!
BUT ONLY LUNALA IS HERE...
IT HAS COMPLETELY DEVOURED SOLGALEO'S AND LUNALA'S ENERGY.
THAT MEANS...
WE MIGHT NEVER SEE DAYLIGHT...
...EVER AGAIN...

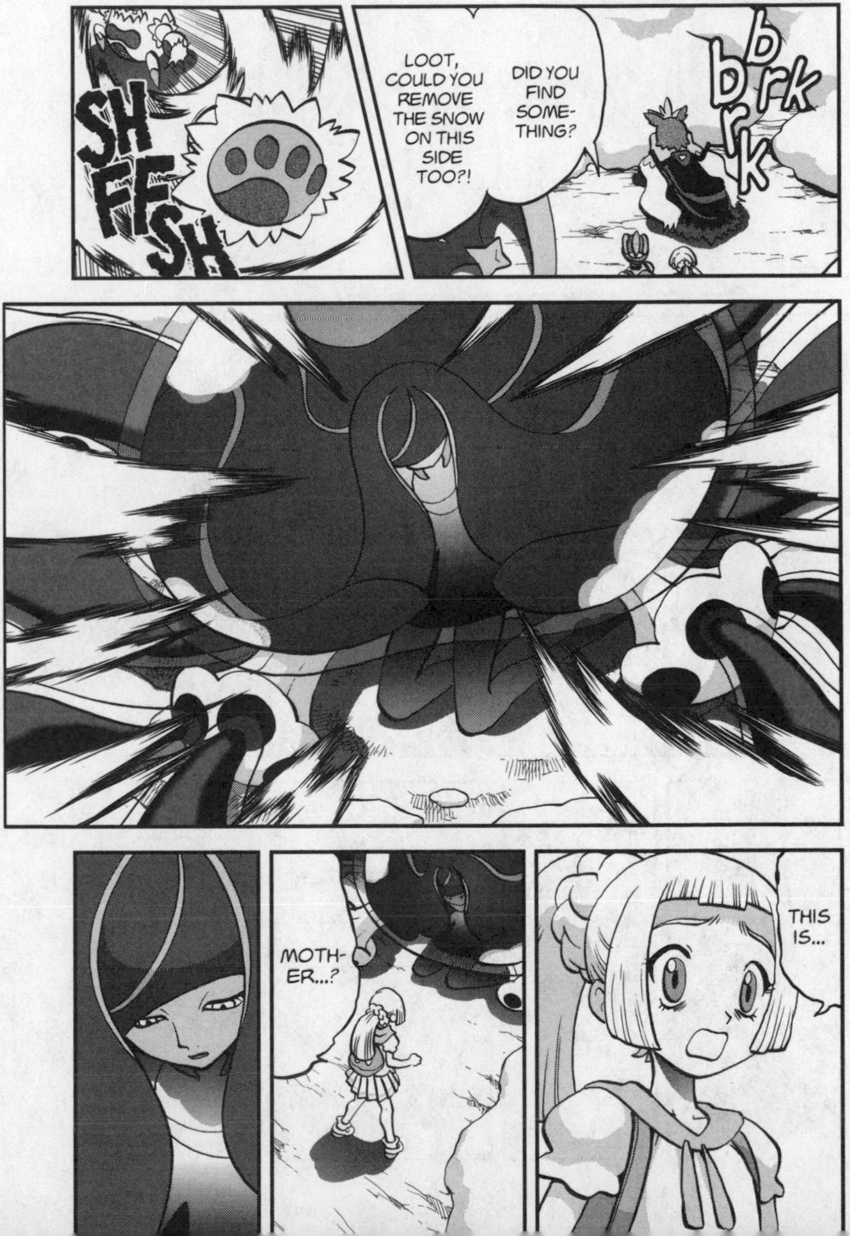
brk brk
DID YOU FIND SOME-THING?
LOOT, COULD YOU REMOVE THE SNOW ON THIS SIDE TOO?!
SHFFSH
THIS IS...
MOTH-ER...?

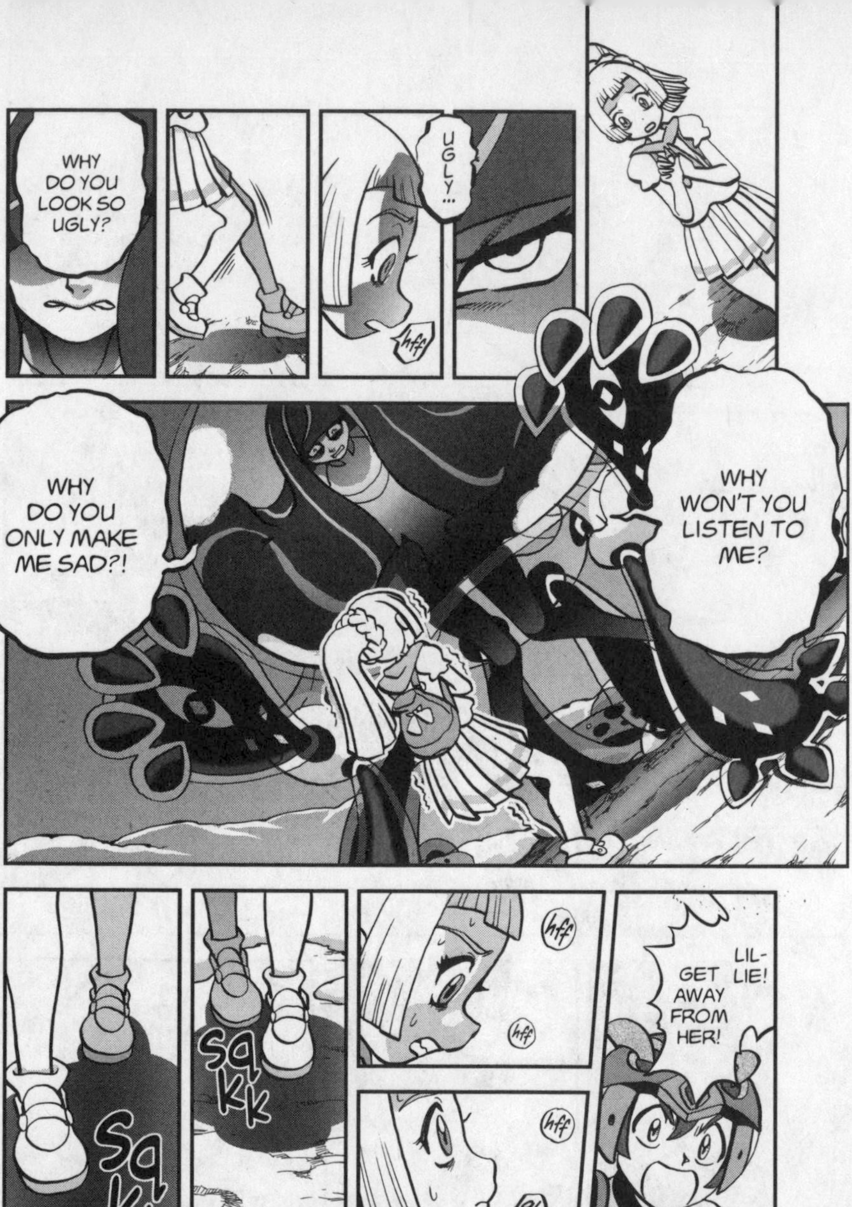
U G L Y...
hff
WHY DO YOU LOOK SO UGLY?
WHY WON'T YOU LISTEN TO ME?
WHY DO YOU ONLY MAKE ME SAD?!
LILLIE! GET AWAY FROM HER!
hff
hff
hff
glp
sqkk
sqkk

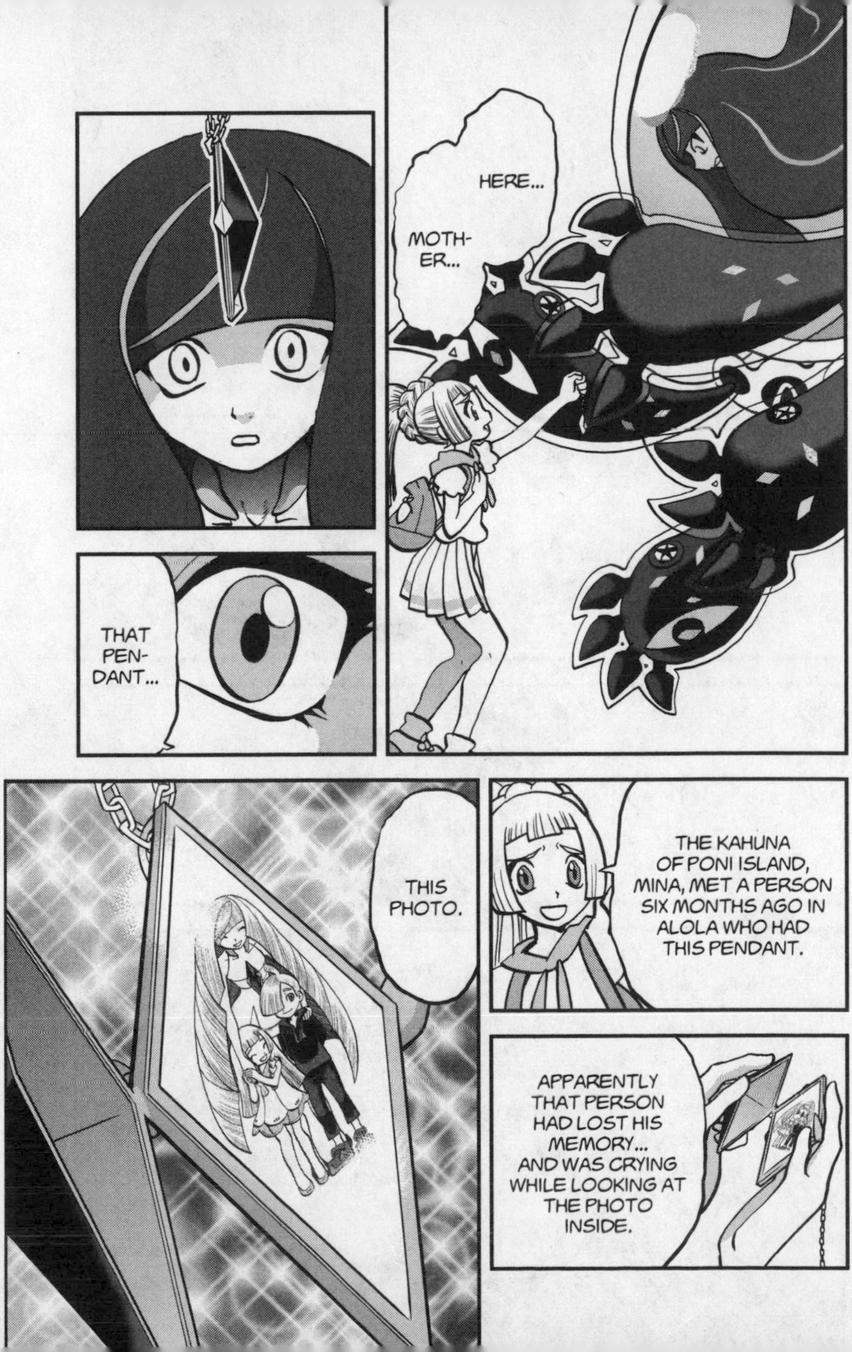
HERE...
MOTHER-ER...
THAT PEN-DANT...
THE KAHUNA OF PONI ISLAND, MINA, MET A PERSON SIX MONTHS AGO IN ALOLA WHO HAD THIS PENDANT.
APPARENTLY THAT PERSON HAD LOST HIS MEMORY... AND WAS CRYING WHILE LOOKING AT THE PHOTO INSIDE.
THIS PHOTO.

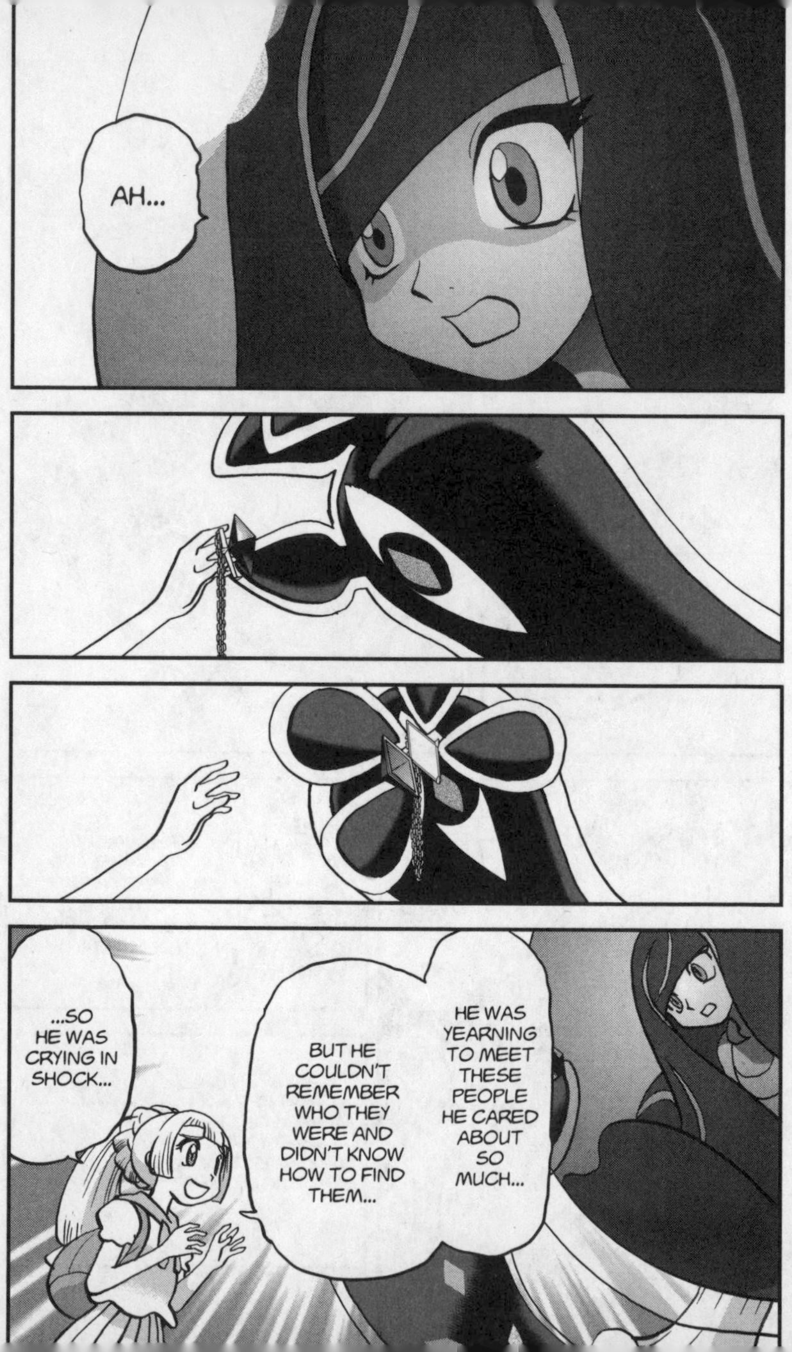
AH...
HE WAS YEARNING TO MEET THESE PEOPLE HE CARED ABOUT SO MUCH...
BUT HE COULDN'T REMEMBER WHO THEY WERE AND DIDN'T KNOW HOW TO FIND THEM...
...SO HE WAS CRYING IN SHOCK...

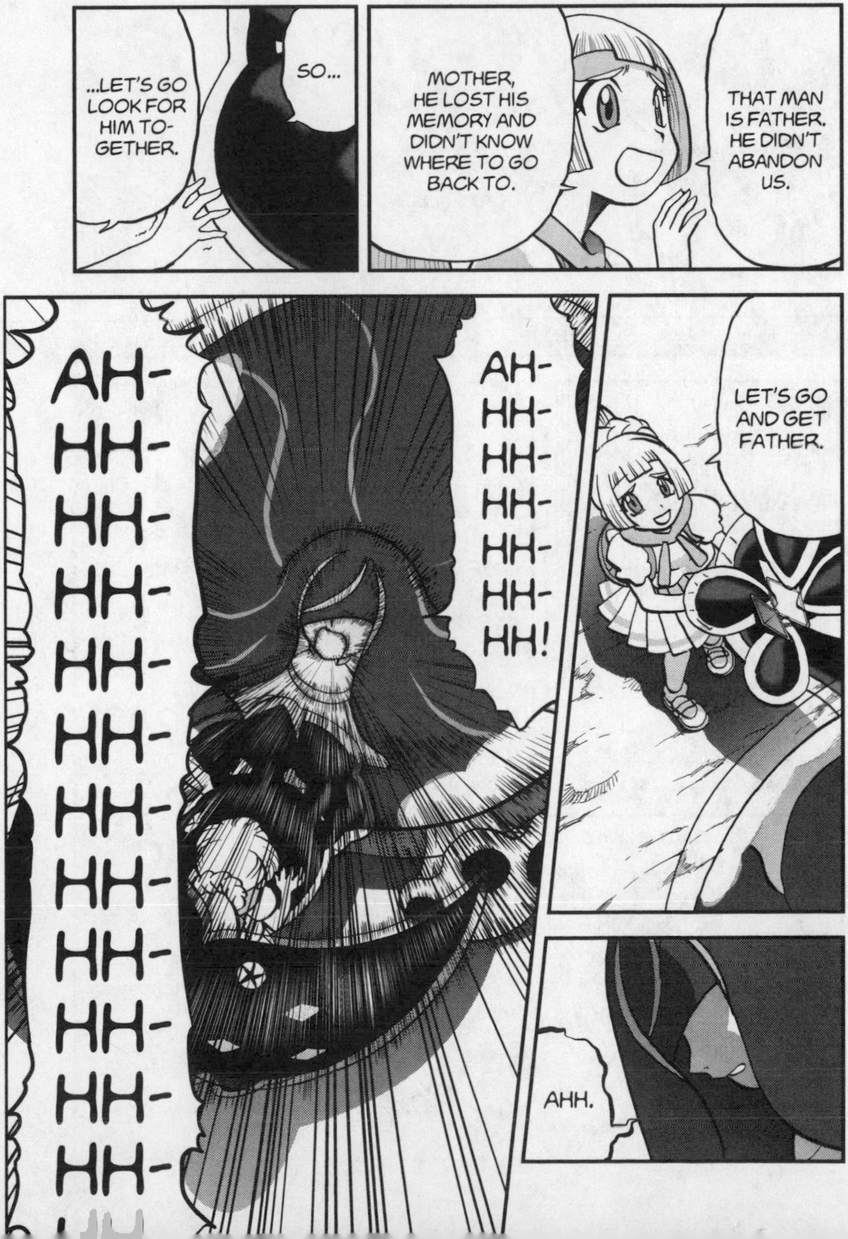
THAT MAN IS FATHER. HE DIDN'T ABANDON US.
MOTHER, HE LOST HIS MEMORY AND DIDN'T KNOW WHERE TO GO BACK TO.
SO...
...LET'S GO LOOK FOR HIM TO-GETHER.
LET'S GO AND GET FATHER.
AHH.
AH-HH-HH-HH-HH-HH-HH!
AH-HH-HH-HH-HH-HH-HH-HH-HH-HH-HH-HH-HH-

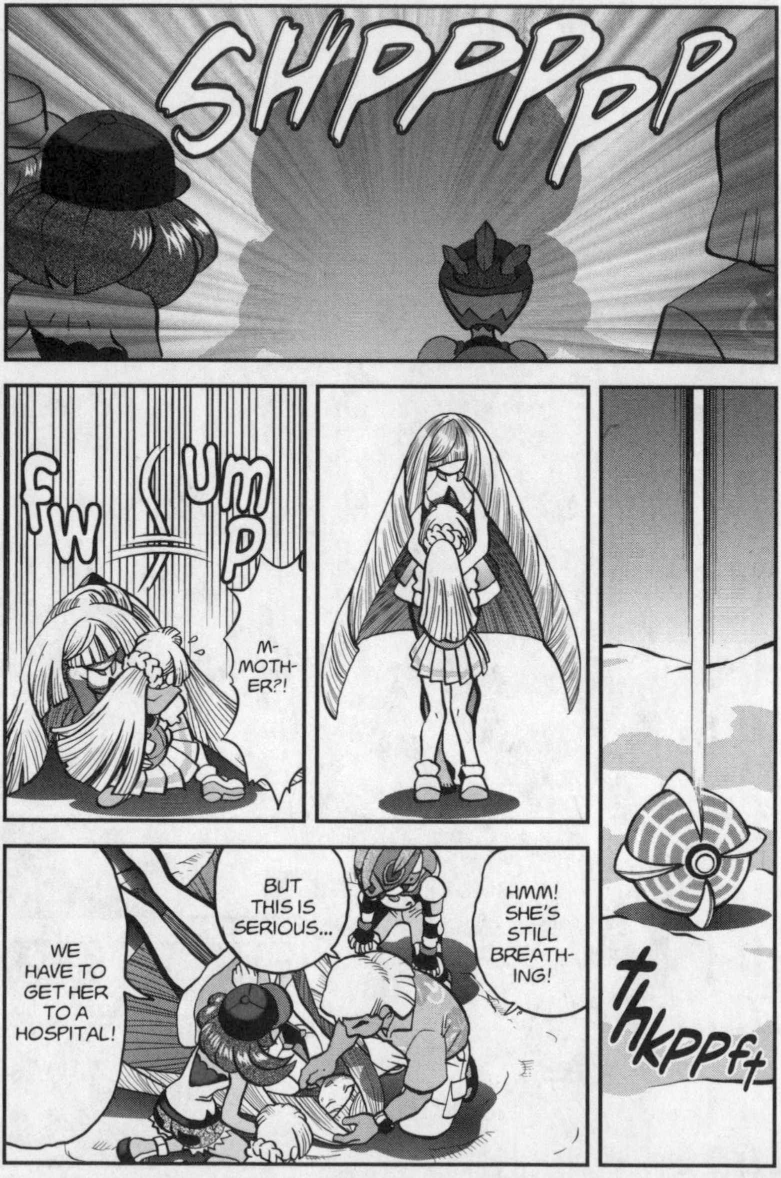
SHPPPPP
thkppft
fwump
M-MOTHER?!
HMM! SHE'S STILL BREATHING!
BUT THIS IS SERIOUS...
WE HAVE TO GET HER TO A HOSPITAL!

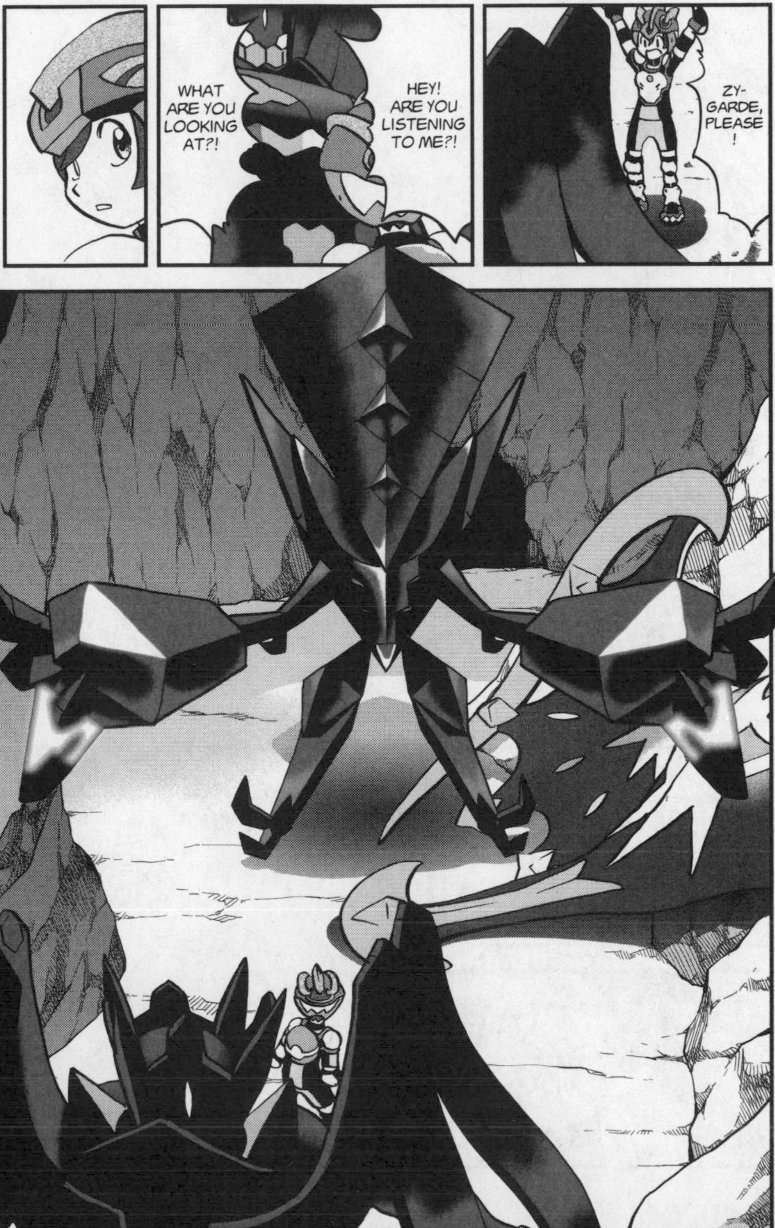
ZY-GARDE, PLEASE!
HEY! ARE YOU LISTENING TO ME?!
WHAT ARE YOU LOOKING AT?!

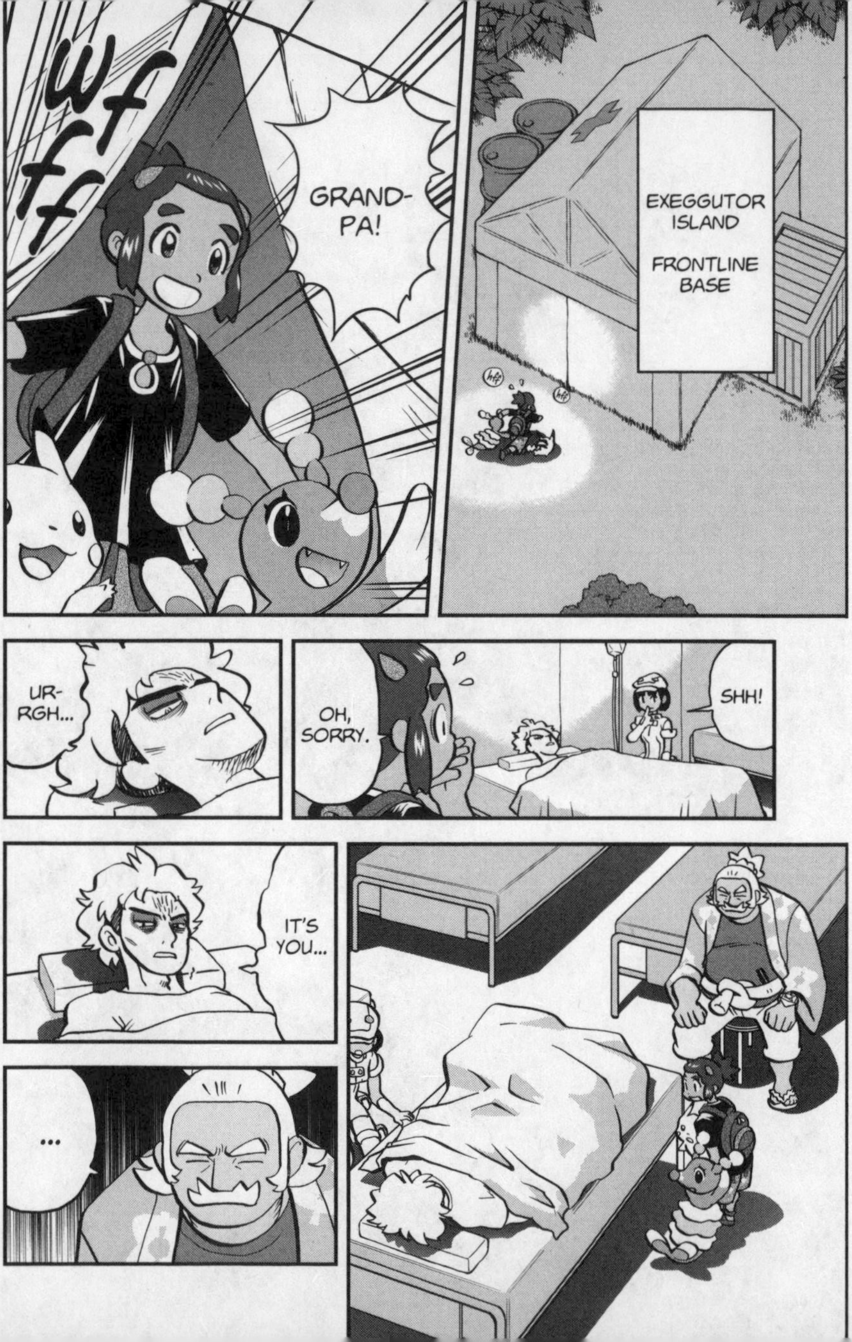
EXEGGUTOR ISLAND

FRONTLINE BASE
wfff
GRAND-PA!
SHH!
OH, SORRY.
UR-RGH...
IT'S YOU...
...

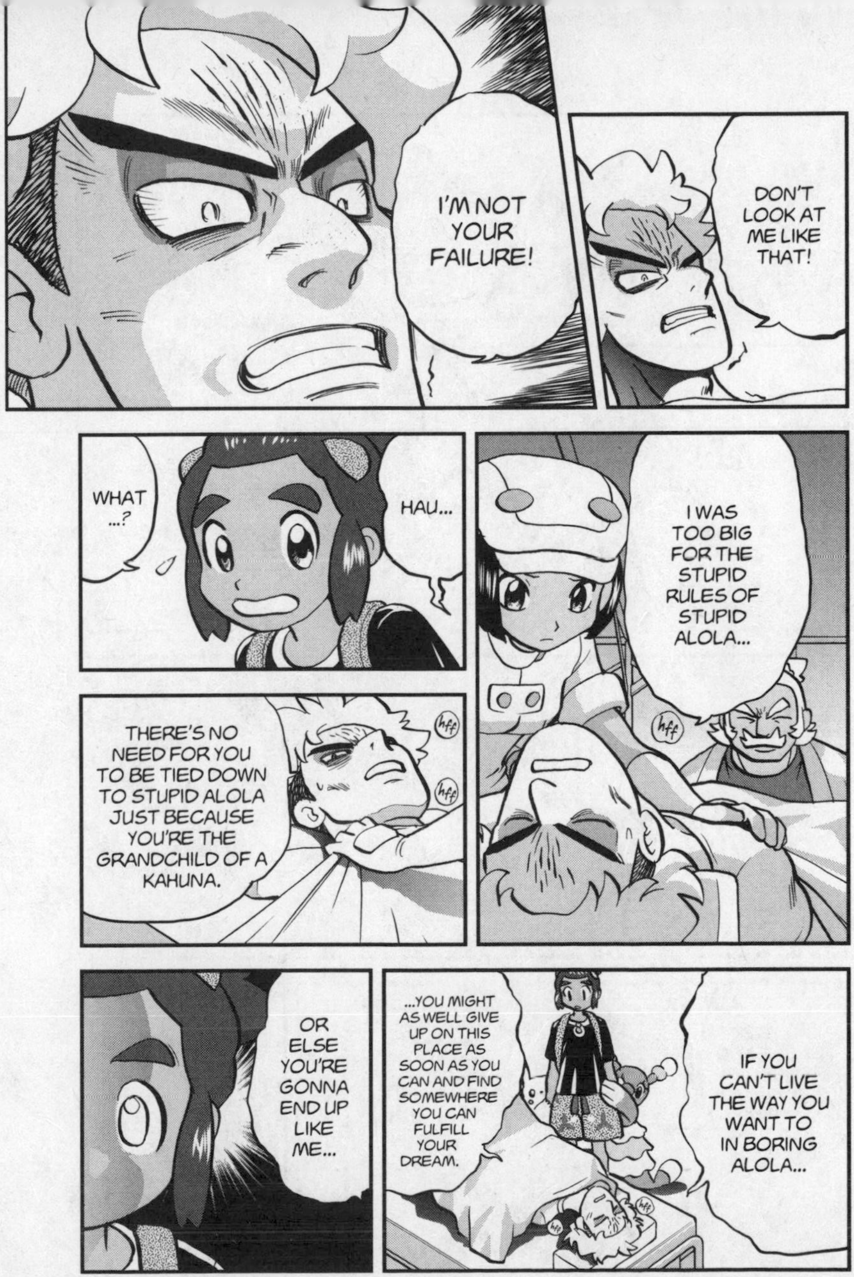
DON'T LOOK AT ME LIKE THAT!
I'M NOT YOUR FAILURE!
I WAS TOO BIG FOR THE STUPID RULES OF STUPID ALOLA...
hff
HAU...
WHAT ...?
hff
hff
THERE'S NO NEED FOR YOU TO BE TIED DOWN TO STUPID ALOLA JUST BECAUSE YOU'RE THE GRANDCHILD OF A KAHUNA.
IF YOU CAN'T LIVE THE WAY YOU WANT TO IN BORING ALOLA...
...YOU MIGHT AS WELL GIVE UP ON THIS PLACE AS SOON AS YOU CAN AND FIND SOMEWHERE YOU CAN FULFILL YOUR DREAM.
hff
hff
OR ELSE YOU'RE GONNA END UP LIKE ME...

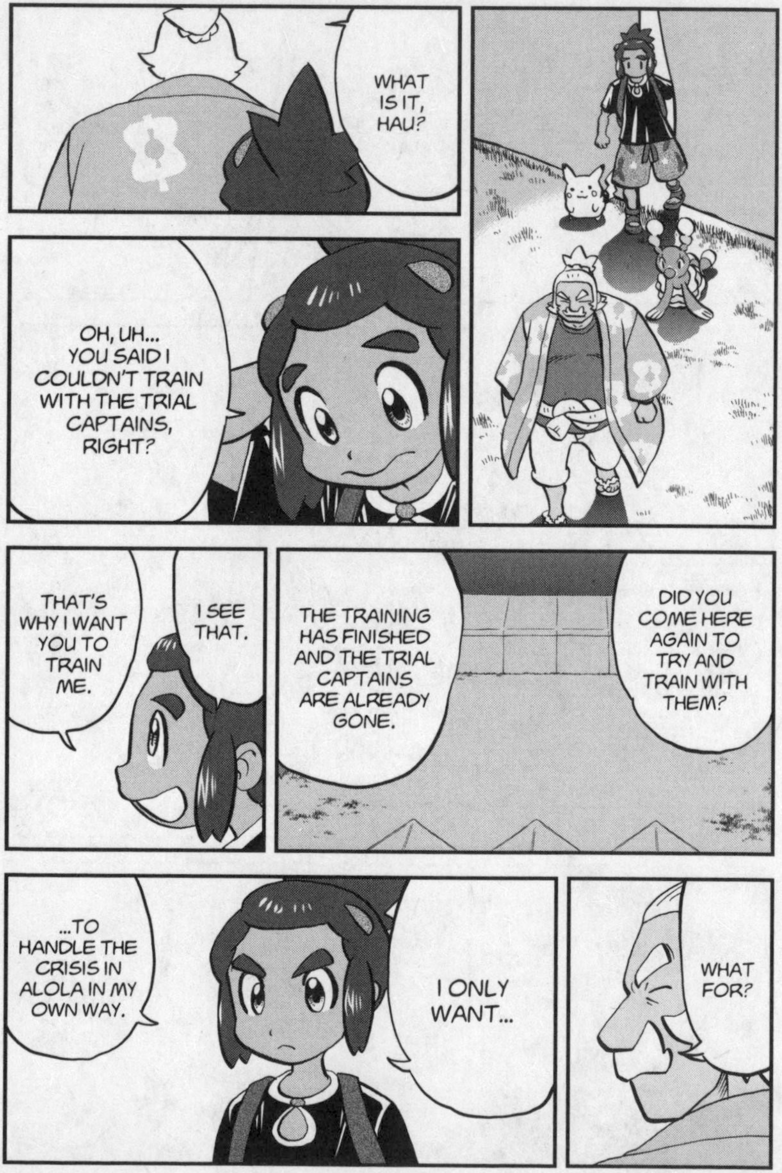
WHAT IS IT, HAU?
OH, UH... YOU SAID I COULDN'T TRAIN WITH THE TRIAL CAPTAINS, RIGHT?
DID YOU COME HERE AGAIN TO TRY AND TRAIN WITH THEM?
THE TRAINING HAS FINISHED AND THE TRIAL CAPTAINS ARE ALREADY GONE.
I SEE THAT.
THAT'S WHY I WANT YOU TO TRAIN ME.
WHAT FOR?
I ONLY WANT...
...TO HANDLE THE CRISIS IN ALOLA IN MY OWN WAY.

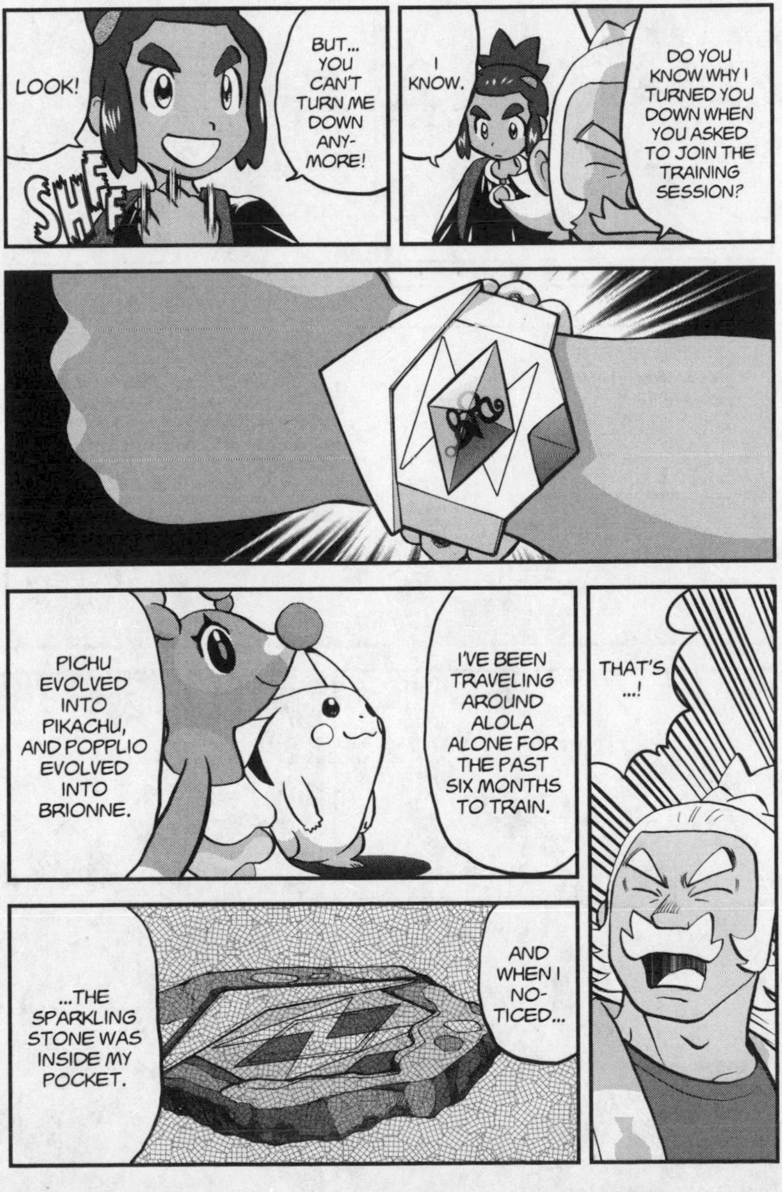
DO YOU KNOW WHY I TURNED YOU DOWN WHEN YOU ASKED TO JOIN THE TRAINING SESSION?
I KNOW.
BUT... YOU CAN'T TURN ME DOWN ANY-MORE!
LOOK!
SHF
THAT'S ...!
I'VE BEEN TRAVELING AROUND ALOLA ALONE FOR THE PAST SIX MONTHS TO TRAIN.
PICHU EVOLVED INTO PIKACHU, AND POPPLIO EVOLVED INTO BRIONNE.
AND WHEN I NO-TICED...
...THE SPARKLING STONE WAS INSIDE MY POCKET.

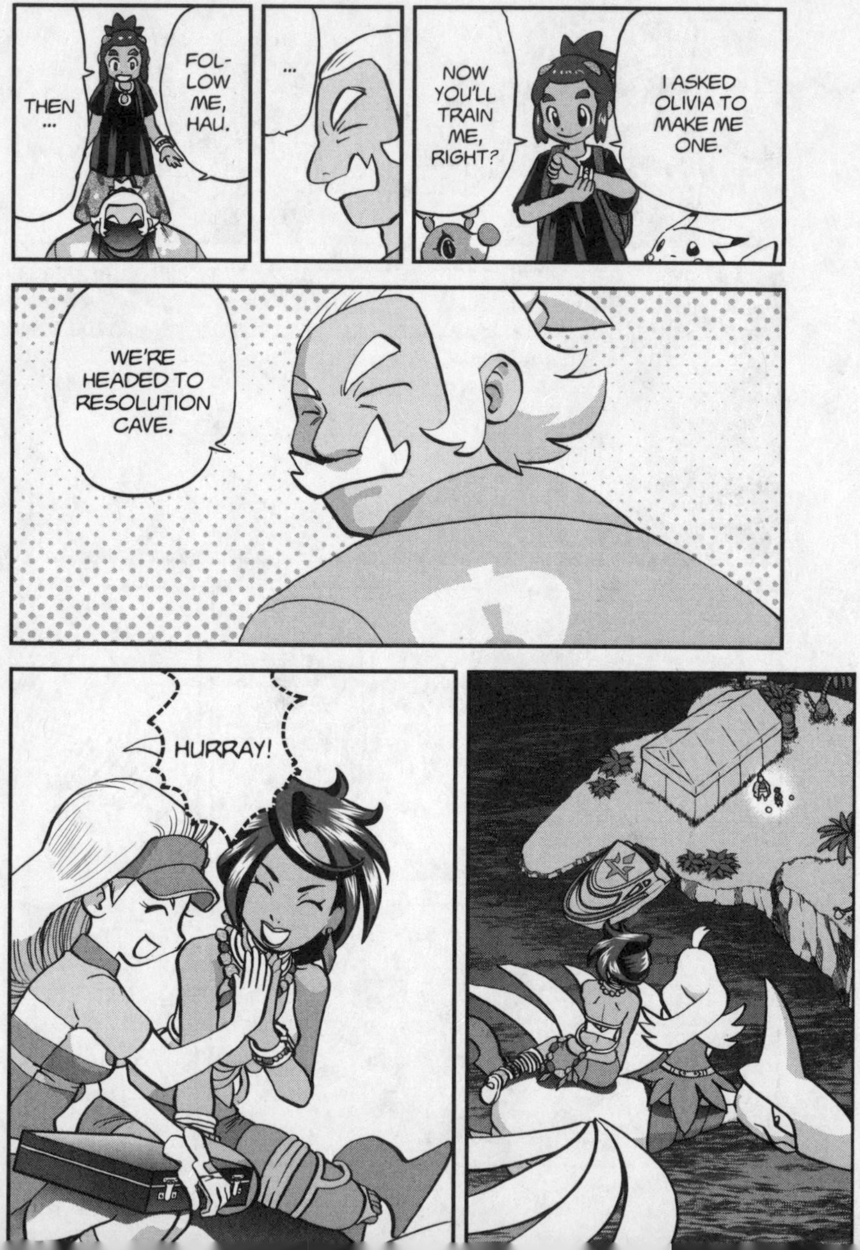
I ASKED OLIVIA TO MAKE ME ONE.
NOW YOU'LL TRAIN ME, RIGHT?
...
FOL-LOW ME, HAU.
THEN ...
WE'RE HEADED TO RESOLUTION CAVE.
HURRAY!

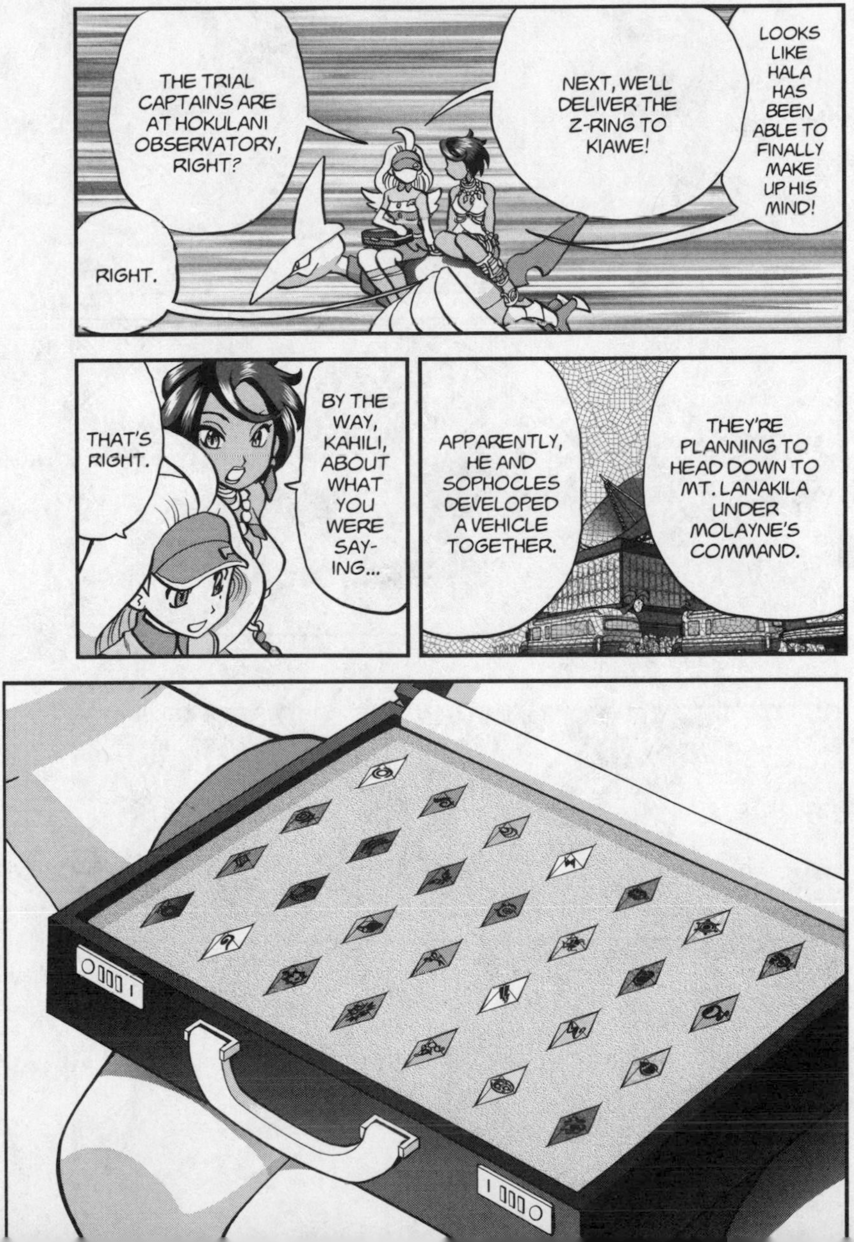

LOOKS LIKE HALA HAS BEEN ABLE TO FINALLY MAKE UP HIS MIND!
NEXT, WE'LL DELIVER THE Z-RING TO KIAWE!
THE TRIAL CAPTAINS ARE AT HOKULANI OBSERVATORY, RIGHT?
RIGHT.
THEY'RE PLANNING TO HEAD DOWN TO MT. LANAKILA UNDER MOLAYNE'S COMMAND.
APPARENTLY, HE AND SOPHOCLES DEVELOPED A VEHICLE TOGETHER.
BY THE WAY, KAHILI, ABOUT WHAT YOU WERE SAYING...
THAT'S RIGHT.

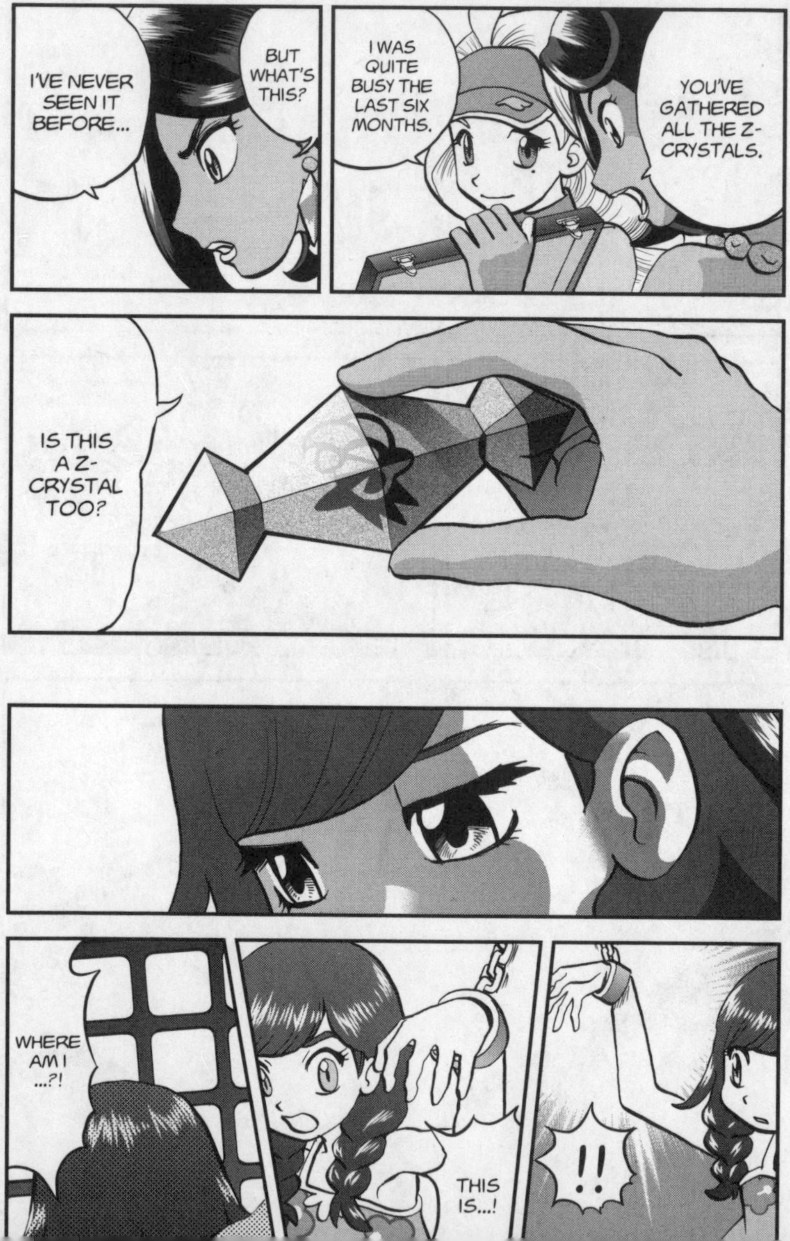
YOU'VE GATHERED ALL THE Z-CRYSTALS.
I WAS QUITE BUSY THE LAST SIX MONTHS.
BUT WHAT'S THIS?
I'VE NEVER SEEN IT BEFORE...
IS THIS A Z-CRYSTAL TOO?
!!
THIS IS...!
WHERE AM I ...?!

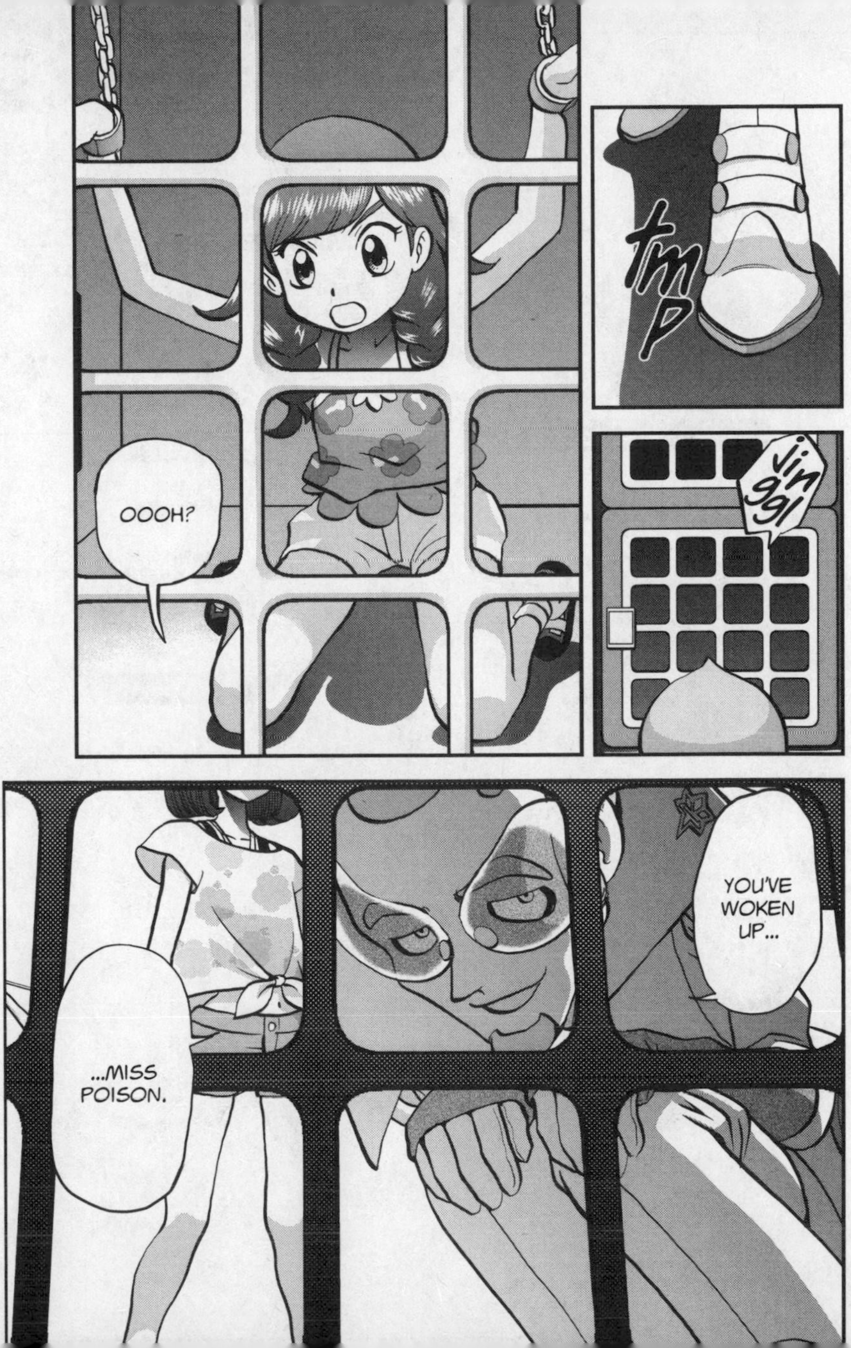
tmp
jinggl
OOOH?
YOU'VE WOKEN UP...
...MISS POISON.

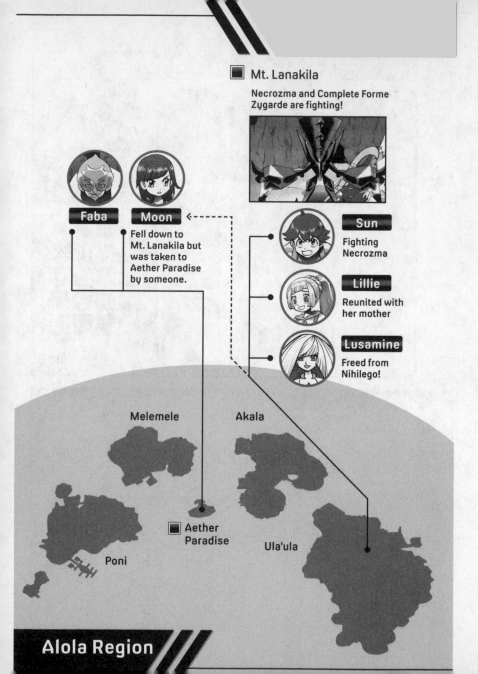

Mt. Lanakila

Necrozma and Complete Forme Zygarde are fighting!

Faba

Moon

Fell down to Mt. Lanakila but was taken to Aether Paradise by someone.

Sun

Fighting Necrozma

Lillie

Reunited with her mother

Lusamine

Freed from Nihilego!

Melemele

Akala

Aether Paradise

Poni

Ula'ula

Alola Region

Adventure 33
Tyrant!! The Fiendish Man!

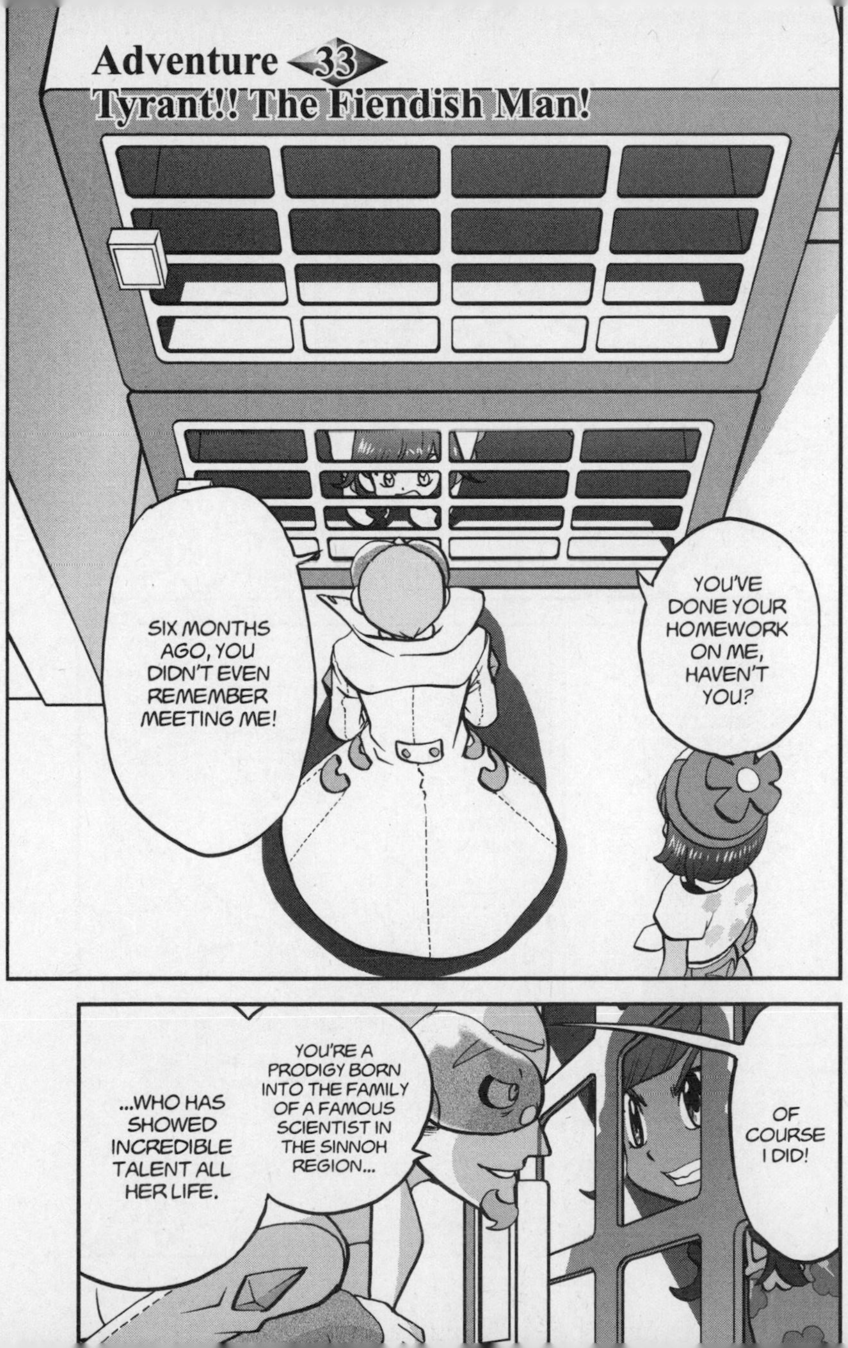
YOU'VE DONE YOUR HOMEWORK ON ME, HAVEN'T YOU?
SIX MONTHS AGO, YOU DIDN'T EVEN REMEMBER MEETING ME!
OF COURSE I DID!
YOU'RE A PRODIGY BORN INTO THE FAMILY OF A FAMOUS SCIENTIST IN THE SINNOH REGION...
...WHO HAS SHOWED INCREDIBLE TALENT ALL HER LIFE.

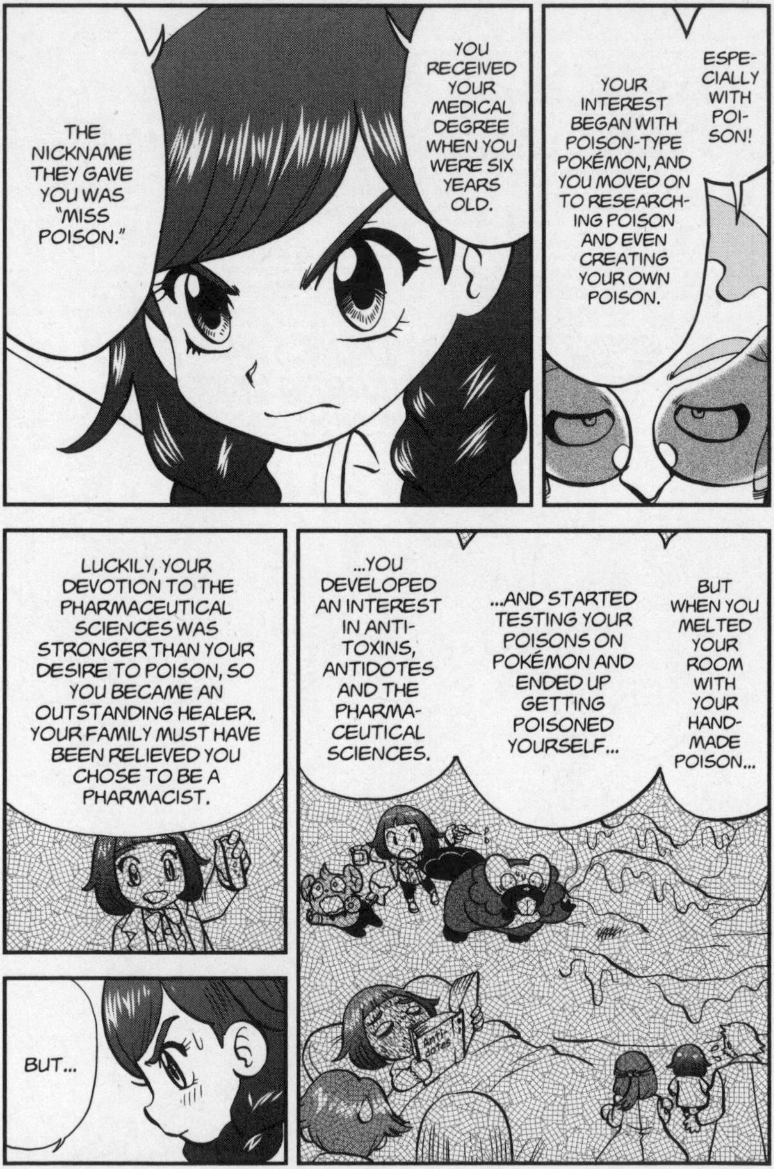
ESPE-CIALLY WITH POI-SON!
YOUR INTEREST BEGAN WITH POISON-TYPE POKÉMON, AND YOU MOVED ON TO RESEARCH-ING POISON AND EVEN CREATING YOUR OWN POISON.
YOU RECEIVED YOUR MEDICAL DEGREE WHEN YOU WERE SIX YEARS OLD.
THE NICKNAME THEY GAVE YOU WAS "MISS POISON."
BUT WHEN YOU MELTED YOUR ROOM WITH YOUR HAND-MADE POISON...
...AND STARTED TESTING YOUR POISONS ON POKÉMON AND ENDED UP GETTING POISONED YOURSELF...
...YOU DEVELOPED AN INTEREST IN ANTI-TOXINS, ANTIDOTES AND THE PHARMA-CEUTICAL SCIENCES.
Anti-dotes
LUCKILY, YOUR DEVOTION TO THE PHARMACEUTICAL SCIENCES WAS STRONGER THAN YOUR DESIRE TO POISON, SO YOU BECAME AN OUTSTANDING HEALER. YOUR FAMILY MUST HAVE BEEN RELIEVED YOU CHOSE TO BE A PHARMACIST.
BUT...

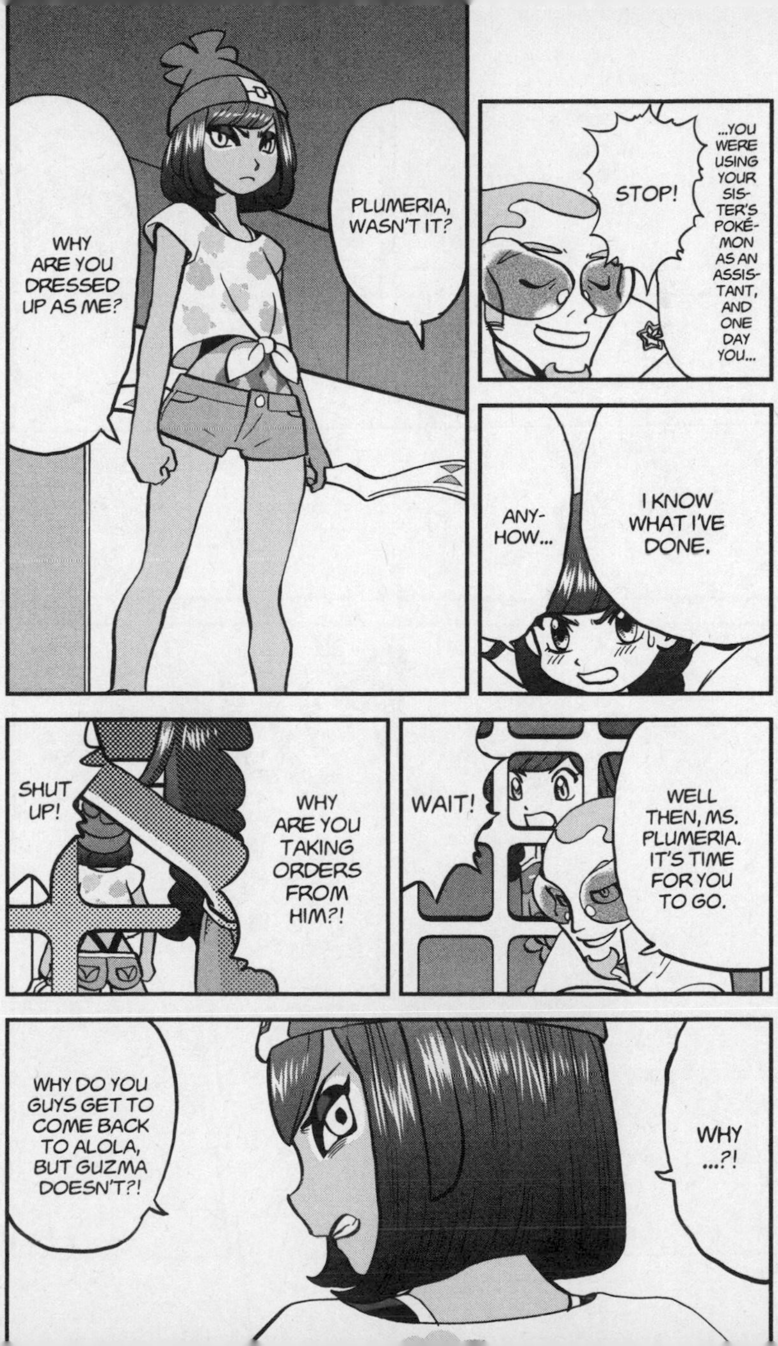
...YOU WERE USING YOUR SISTER'S POKÉMON AS AN ASSISTANT, AND ONE DAY YOU...
STOP!
I KNOW WHAT I'VE DONE.
ANYHOW...
PLUMERIA, WASN'T IT?
WHY ARE YOU DRESSED UP AS ME?
WELL THEN, MS. PLUMERIA. IT'S TIME FOR YOU TO GO.
WAIT!
WHY ARE YOU TAKING ORDERS FROM HIM?!
SHUT UP!
WHY ...?!
WHY DO YOU GUYS GET TO COME BACK TO ALOLA, BUT GUZMA DOESN'T?!

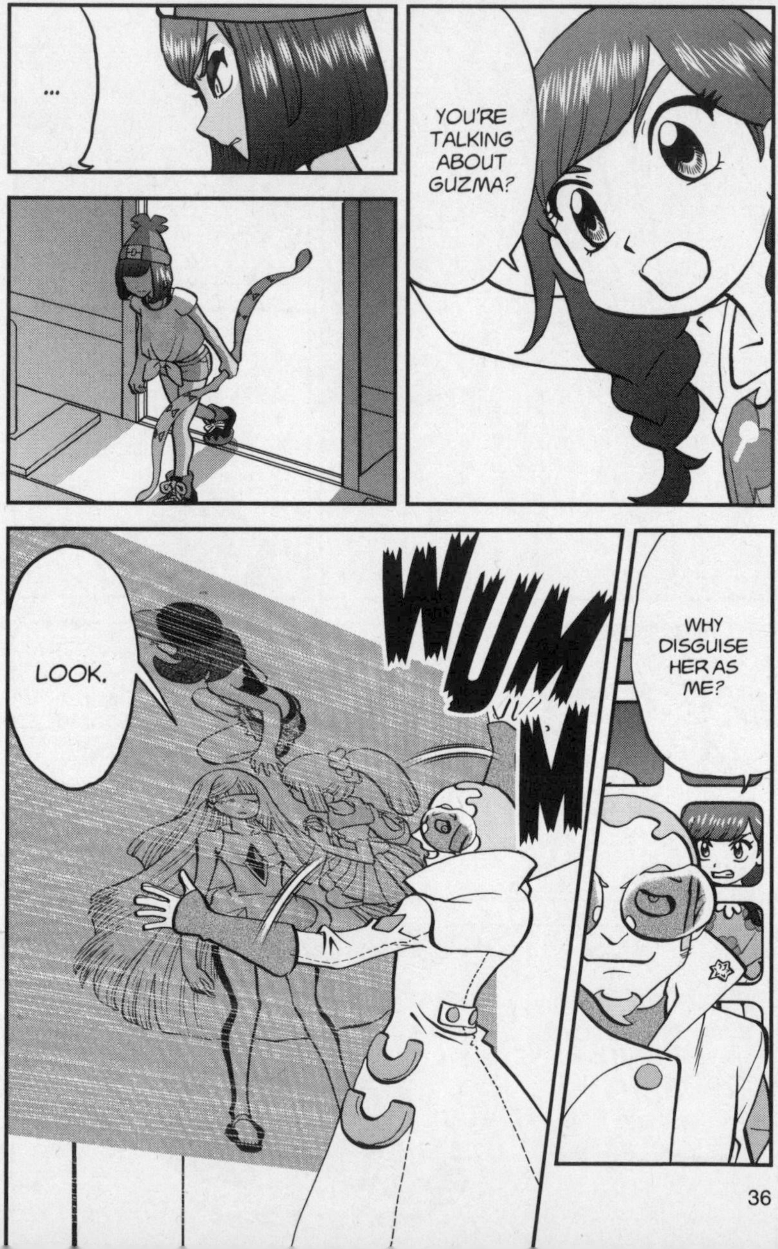
YOU'RE TALKING ABOUT GUZMA?
...
WHY DISGUISE HER AS ME?
WUMM
LOOK.

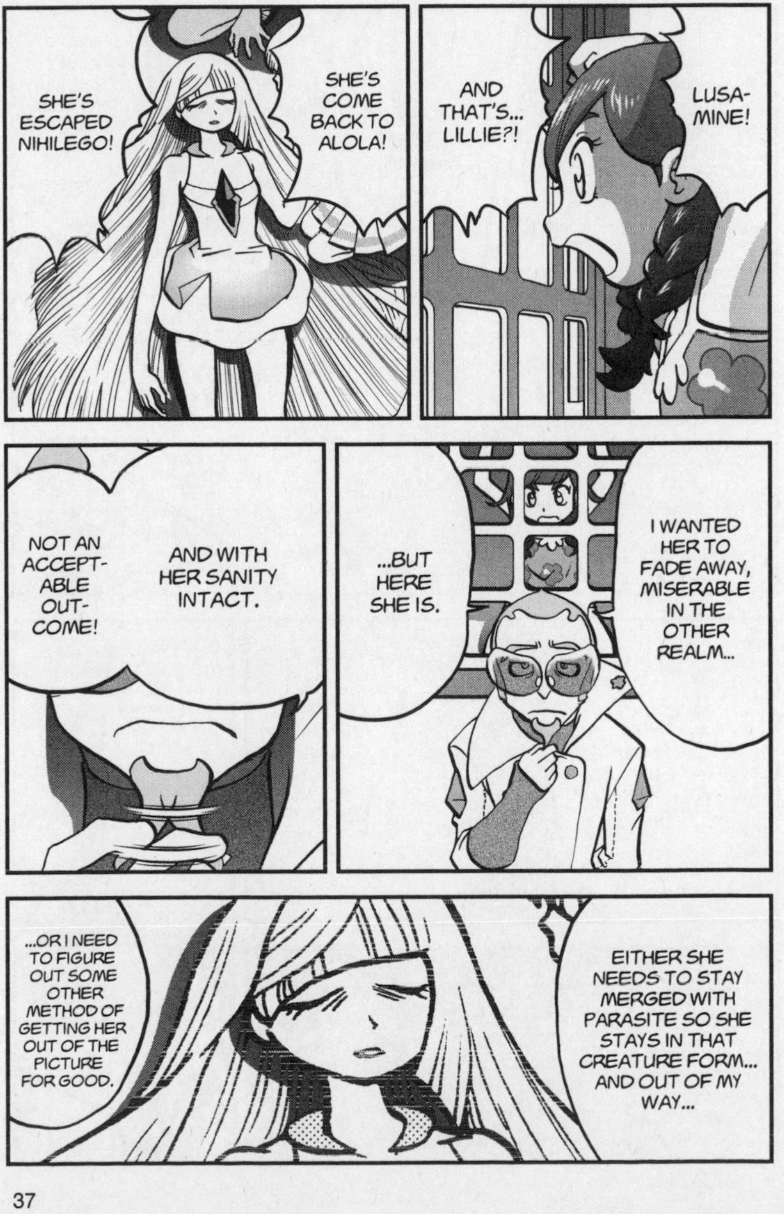
LUSA-MINE!
AND THAT'S... LILLIE?!
SHE'S COME BACK TO ALOLA!
SHE'S ESCAPED NIHILEGO!
I WANTED HER TO FADE AWAY, MISERABLE IN THE OTHER REALM...
...BUT HERE SHE IS.
AND WITH HER SANITY INTACT.
NOT AN ACCEPT-ABLE OUT-COME!
EITHER SHE NEEDS TO STAY MERGED WITH PARASITE SO SHE STAYS IN THAT CREATURE FORM... AND OUT OF MY WAY...
...OR I NEED TO FIGURE OUT SOME OTHER METHOD OF GETTING HER OUT OF THE PICTURE FOR GOOD.

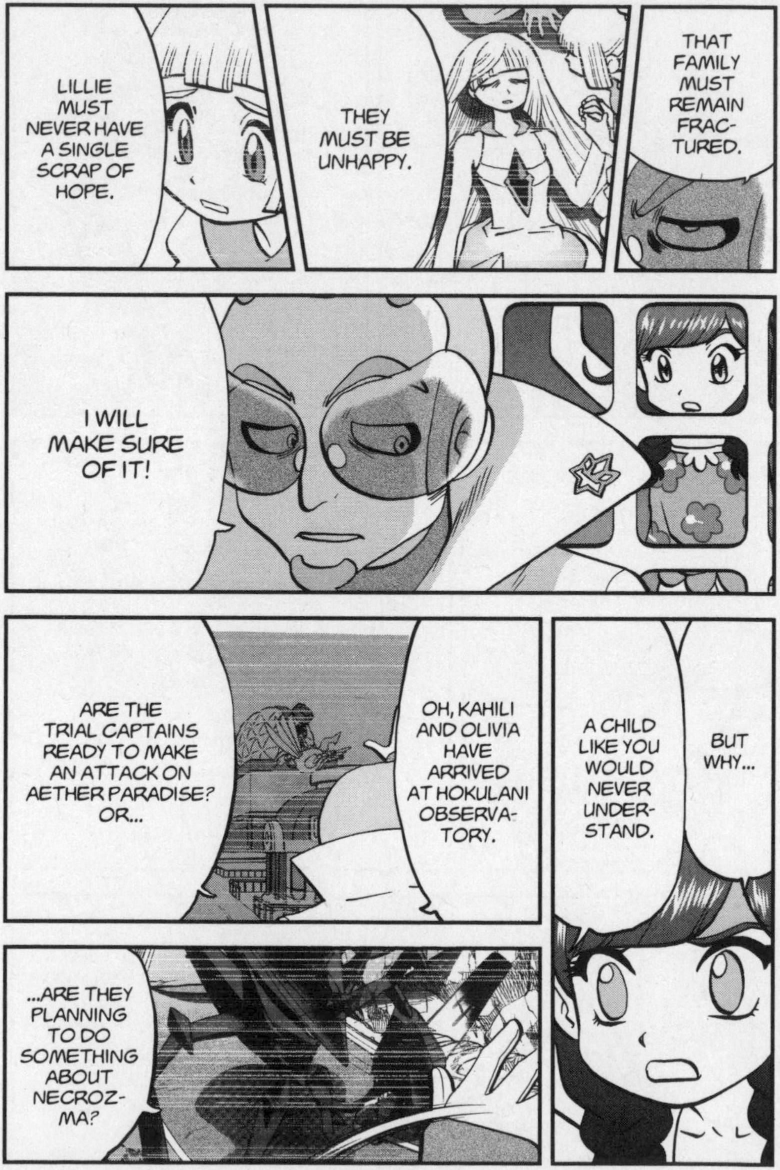
THAT FAMILY MUST REMAIN FRAC-TURED.
THEY MUST BE UNHAPPY.
LILLIE MUST NEVER HAVE A SINGLE SCRAP OF HOPE.
I WILL MAKE SURE OF IT!
BUT WHY...
A CHILD LIKE YOU WOULD NEVER UNDER-STAND.
OH, KAHILI AND OLIVIA HAVE ARRIVED AT HOKULANI OBSERVA-TORY.
ARE THE TRIAL CAPTAINS READY TO MAKE AN ATTACK ON AETHER PARADISE? OR...
...ARE THEY PLANNING TO DO SOMETHING ABOUT NECROZ-MA?

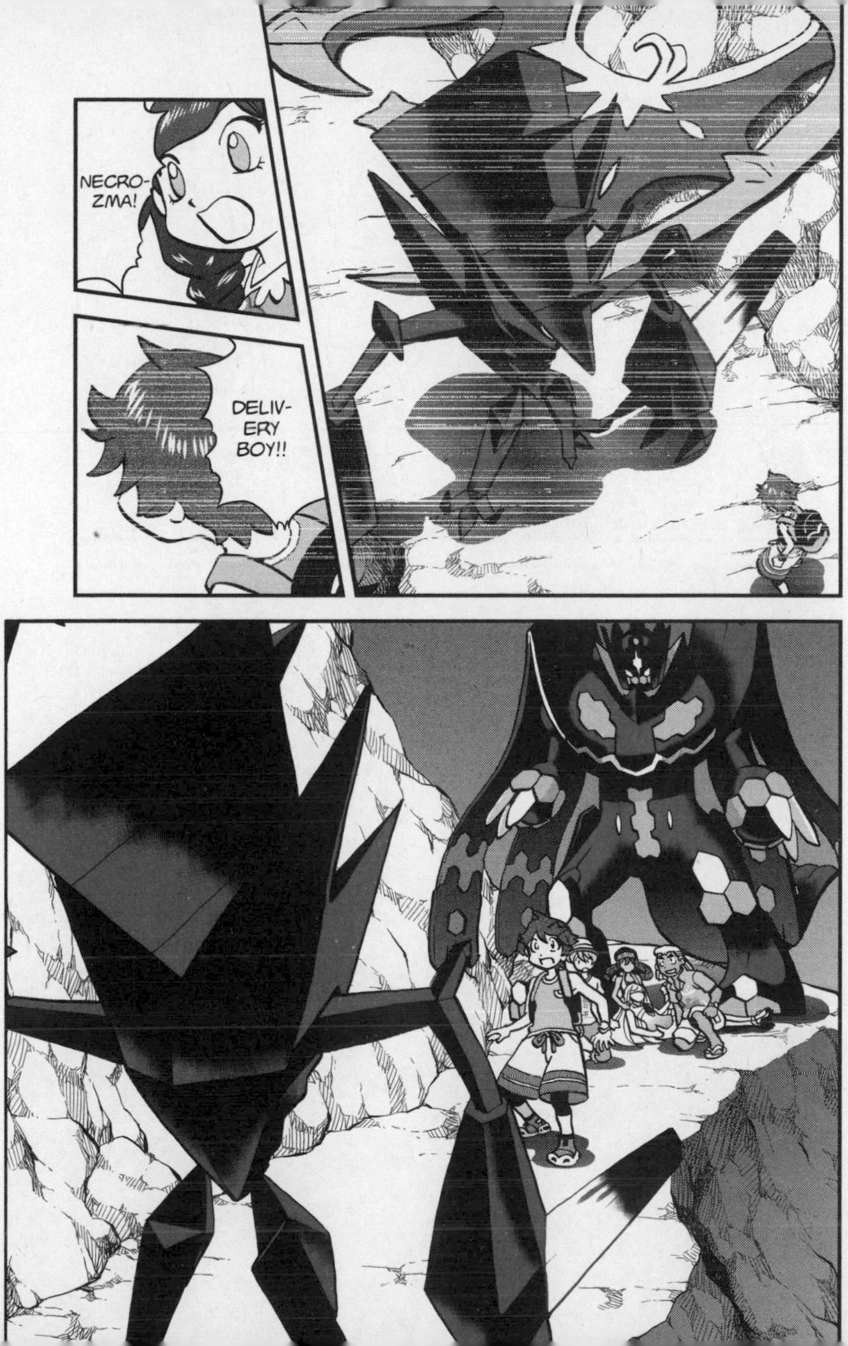
NECRO-
ZMA!
DELIV-
ERY
BOY!!

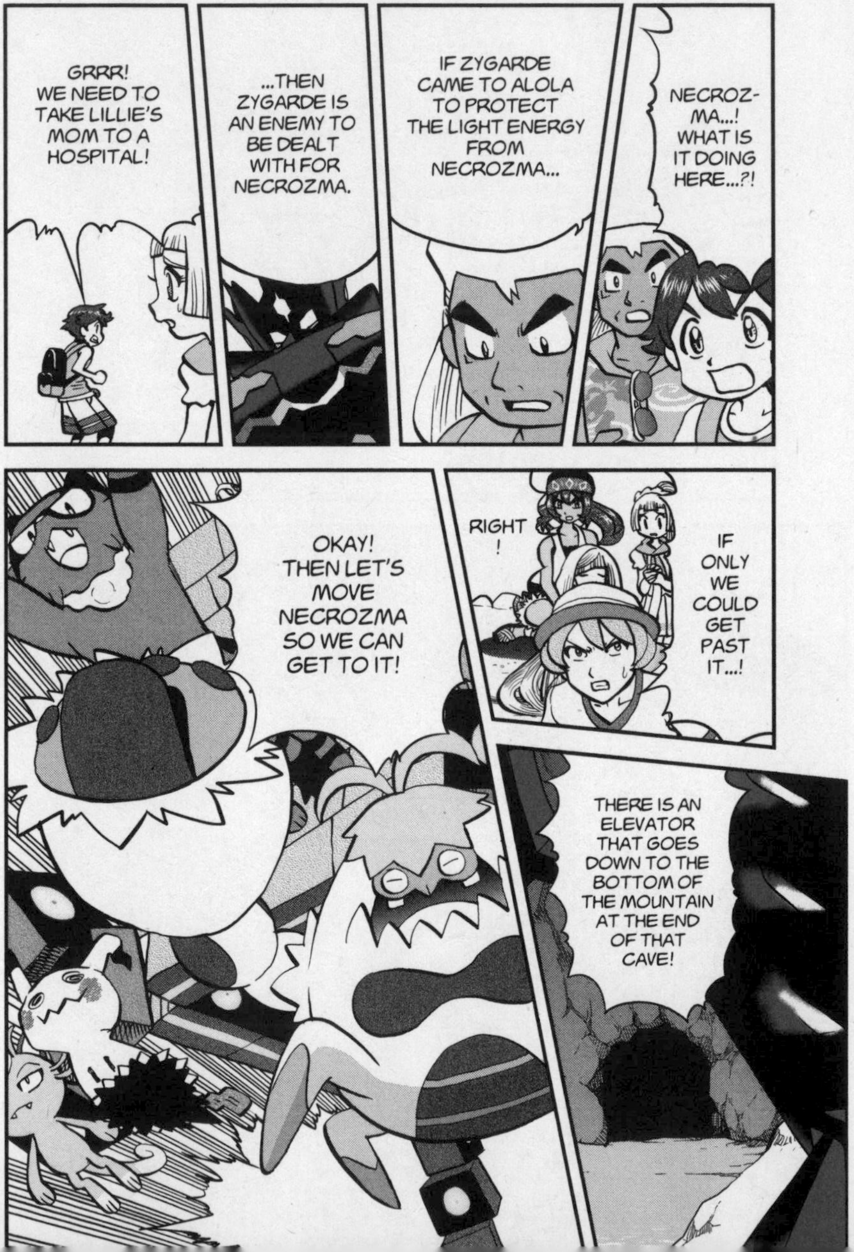
NECROZ-MA...! WHAT IS IT DOING HERE...?!
IF ZYGARDE CAME TO ALOLA TO PROTECT THE LIGHT ENERGY FROM NECROZMA...
...THEN ZYGARDE IS AN ENEMY TO BE DEALT WITH FOR NECROZMA.
GRRR! WE NEED TO TAKE LILLIE'S MOM TO A HOSPITAL!
IF ONLY WE COULD GET PAST IT...!
RIGHT!
THERE IS AN ELEVATOR THAT GOES DOWN TO THE BOTTOM OF THE MOUNTAIN AT THE END OF THAT CAVE!
OKAY! THEN LET'S MOVE NECROZMA SO WE CAN GET TO IT!

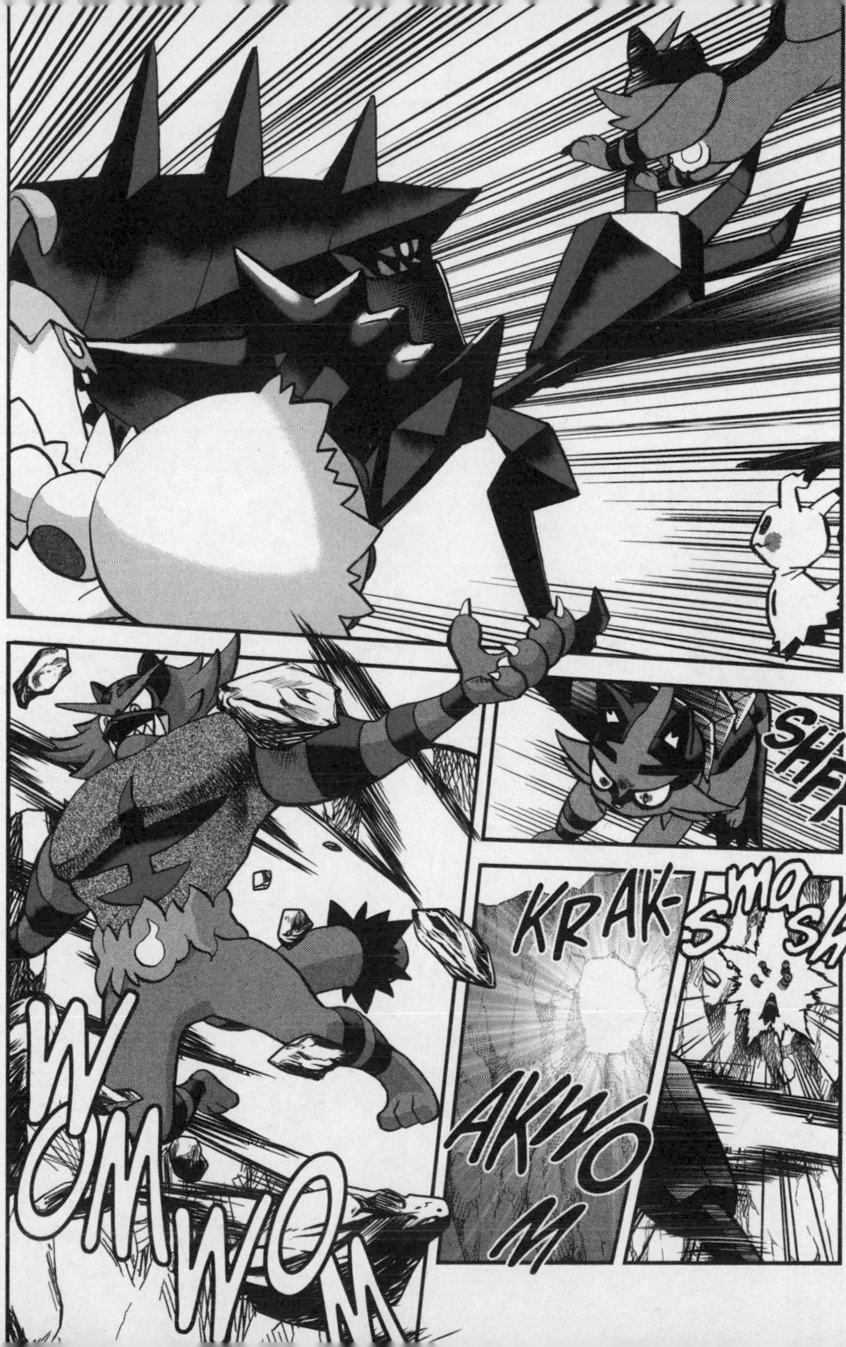
SHFF
KRAK-SMASH
AKWOMM
WOMWOM

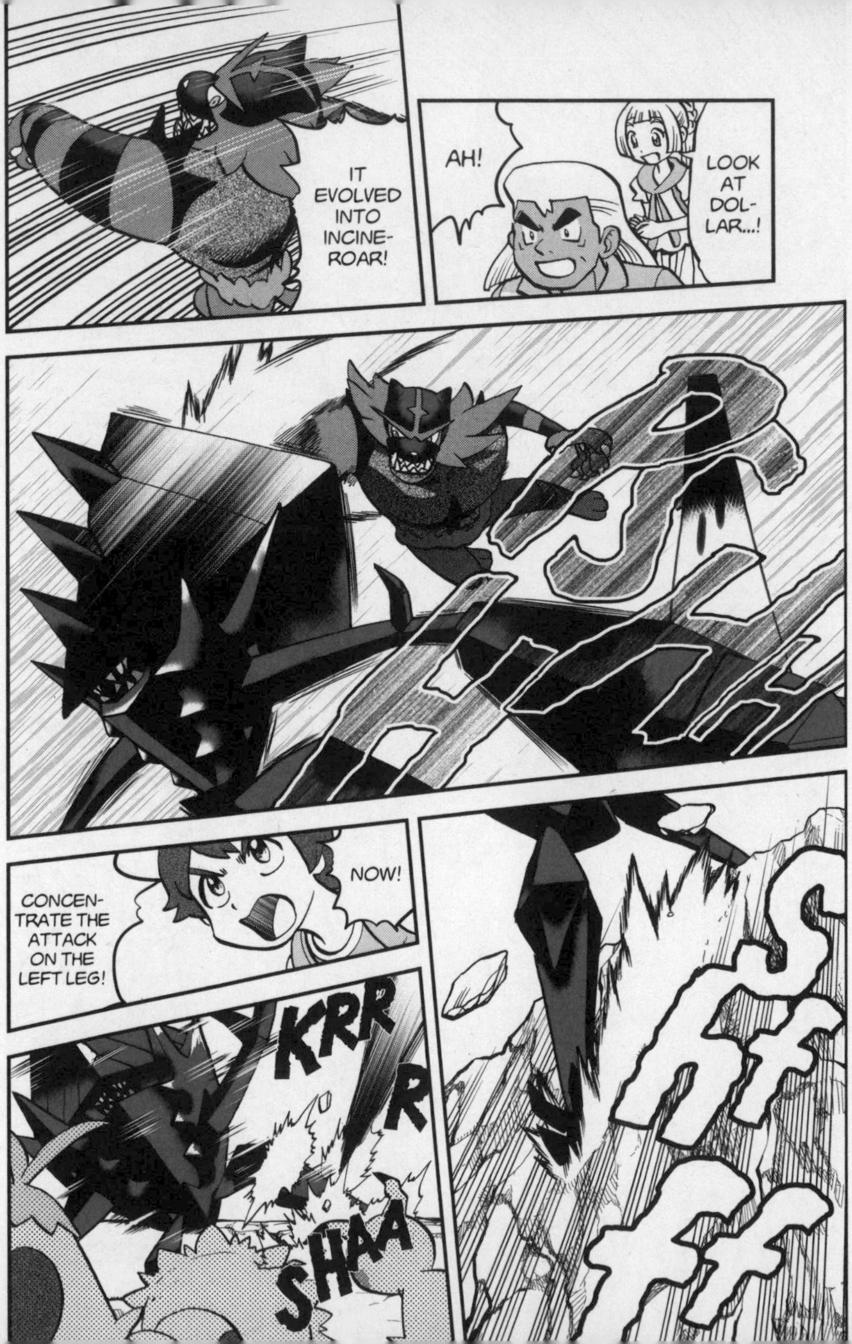
LOOK AT DOL-LAR...!
AH!
IT EVOLVED INTO INCINE-ROAR!
NOW!
CONCEN-TRATE THE ATTACK ON THE LEFT LEG!
KRRR
SHAA

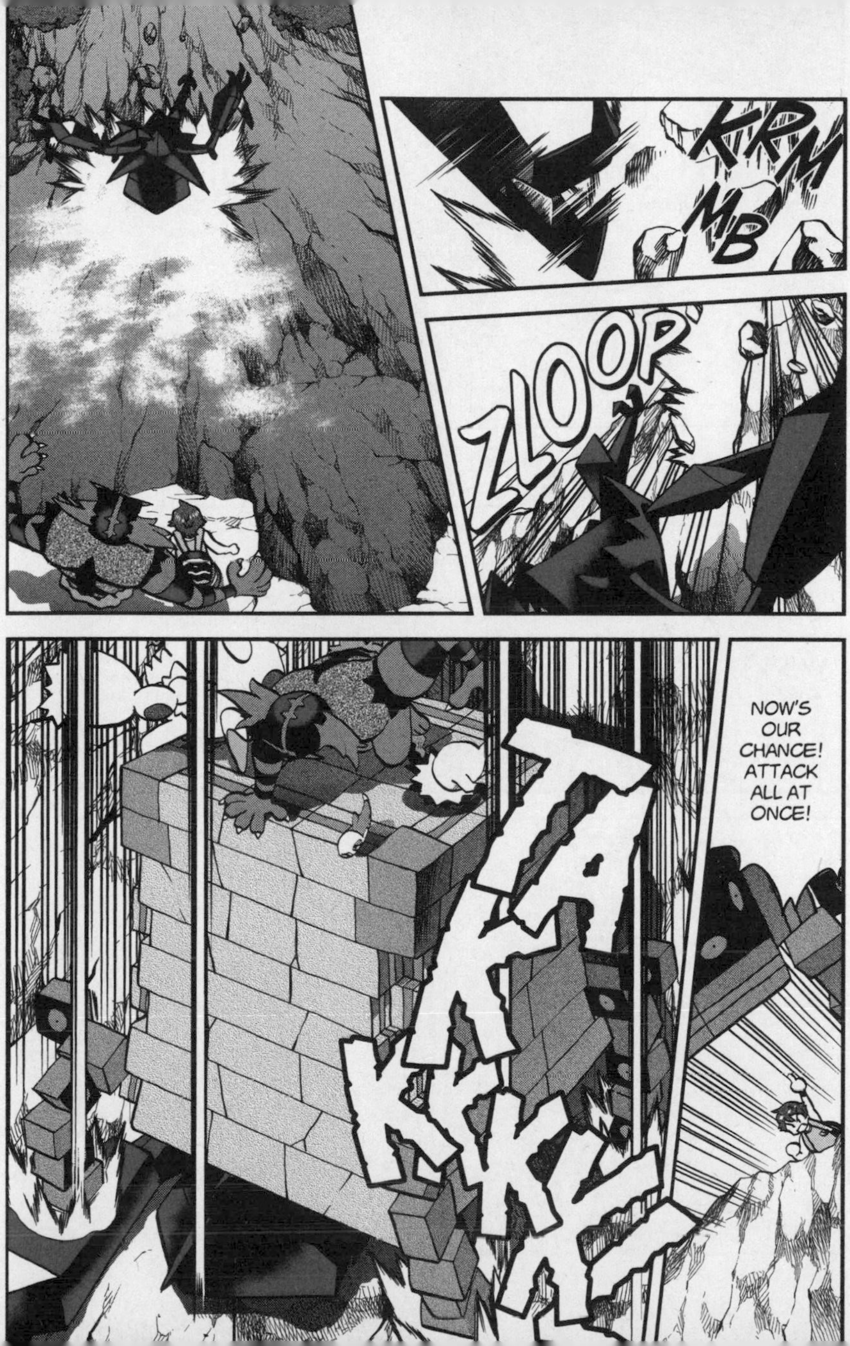
KRMMB
ZLOOP
NOW'S OUR CHANCE! ATTACK ALL AT ONCE!
TAKKA

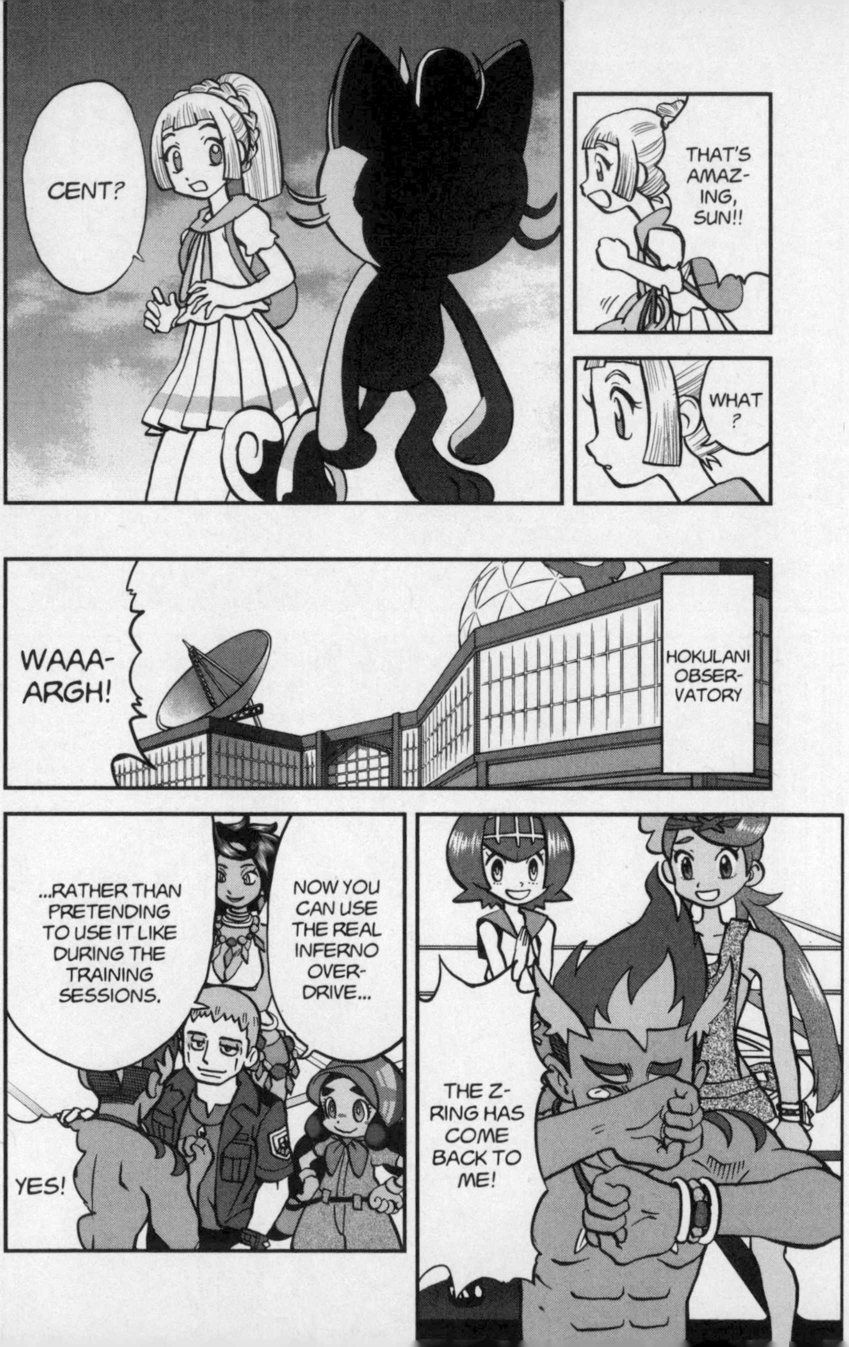
THAT'S AMAZ-ING, SUN!!
WHAT?
CENT?
HOKULANI OBSERVATORY
WAAA-ARGH!
THE Z-RING HAS COME BACK TO ME!
NOW YOU CAN USE THE REAL INFERNO OVERDRIVE...
...RATHER THAN PRETENDING TO USE IT LIKE DURING THE TRAINING SESSIONS.
YES!

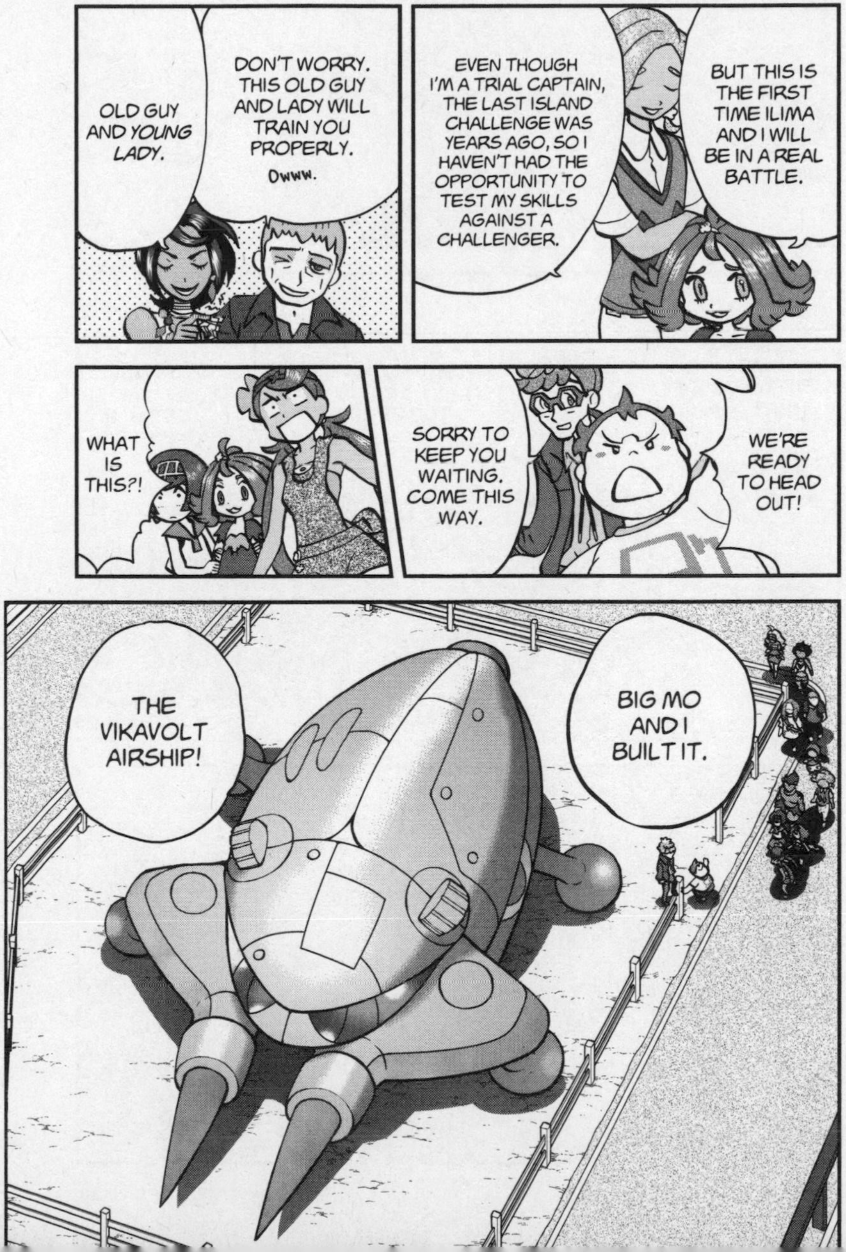
BUT THIS IS THE FIRST TIME ILIMA AND I WILL BE IN A REAL BATTLE.
EVEN THOUGH I'M A TRIAL CAPTAIN, THE LAST ISLAND CHALLENGE WAS YEARS AGO, SO I HAVEN'T HAD THE OPPORTUNITY TO TEST MY SKILLS AGAINST A CHALLENGER.
DON'T WORRY. THIS OLD GUY AND LADY WILL TRAIN YOU PROPERLY.
Owww.
OLD GUY AND *YOUNG* LADY.
WE'RE READY TO HEAD OUT!
SORRY TO KEEP YOU WAITING. COME THIS WAY.
WHAT IS THIS?!
BIG MO AND I BUILT IT.
THE VIKAVOLT AIRSHIP!

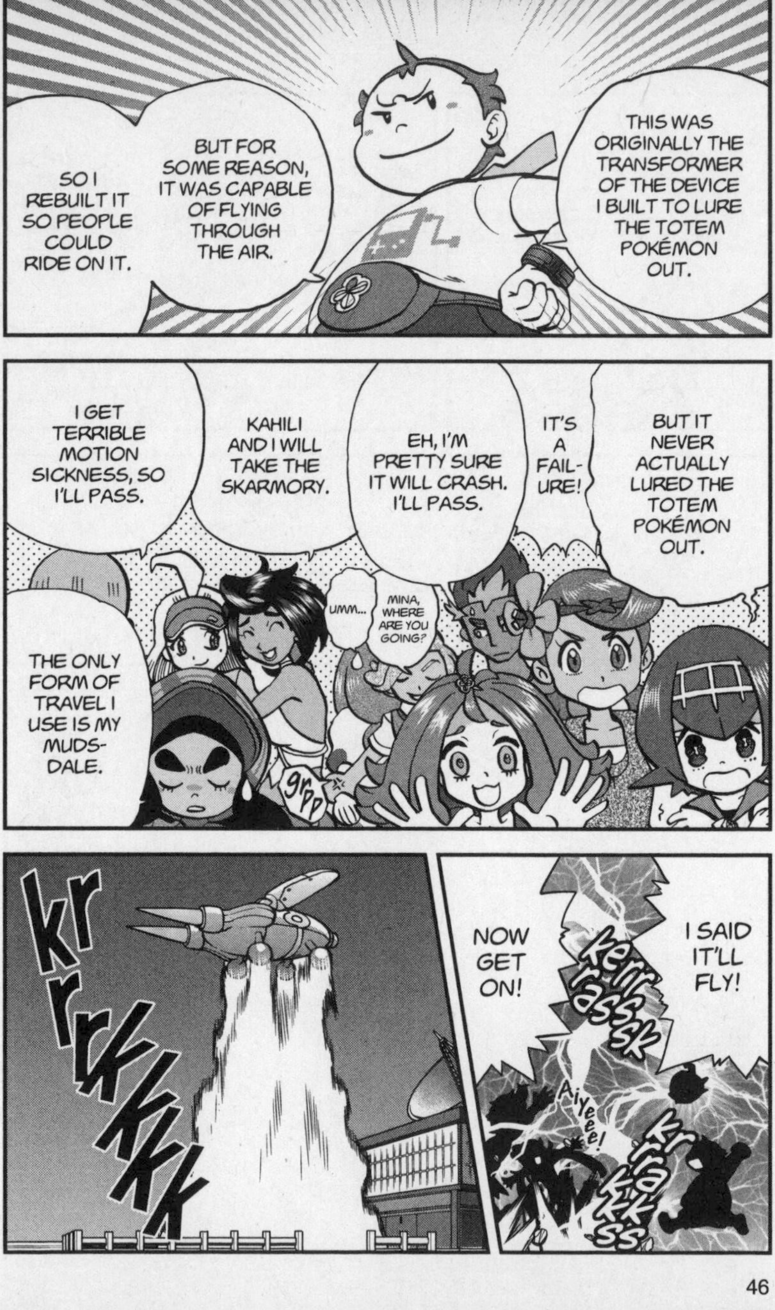
THIS WAS ORIGINALLY THE TRANSFORMER OF THE DEVICE I BUILT TO LURE THE TOTEM POKÉMON OUT.
BUT FOR SOME REASON, IT WAS CAPABLE OF FLYING THROUGH THE AIR.
SO I REBUILT IT SO PEOPLE COULD RIDE ON IT.
BUT IT NEVER ACTUALLY LURED THE TOTEM POKÉMON OUT.
IT'S A FAIL-URE!
EH, I'M PRETTY SURE IT WILL CRASH. I'LL PASS.
KAHILI AND I WILL TAKE THE SKARMORY.
I GET TERRIBLE MOTION SICKNESS, SO I'LL PASS.
MINA, WHERE ARE YOU GOING?
UMM...
THE ONLY FORM OF TRAVEL I USE IS MY MUDS-DALE.
grpp
I SAID IT'LL FLY!
NOW GET ON!
kerrrasssk
Aiyeee!
krrrakkss
krrrKKKKK

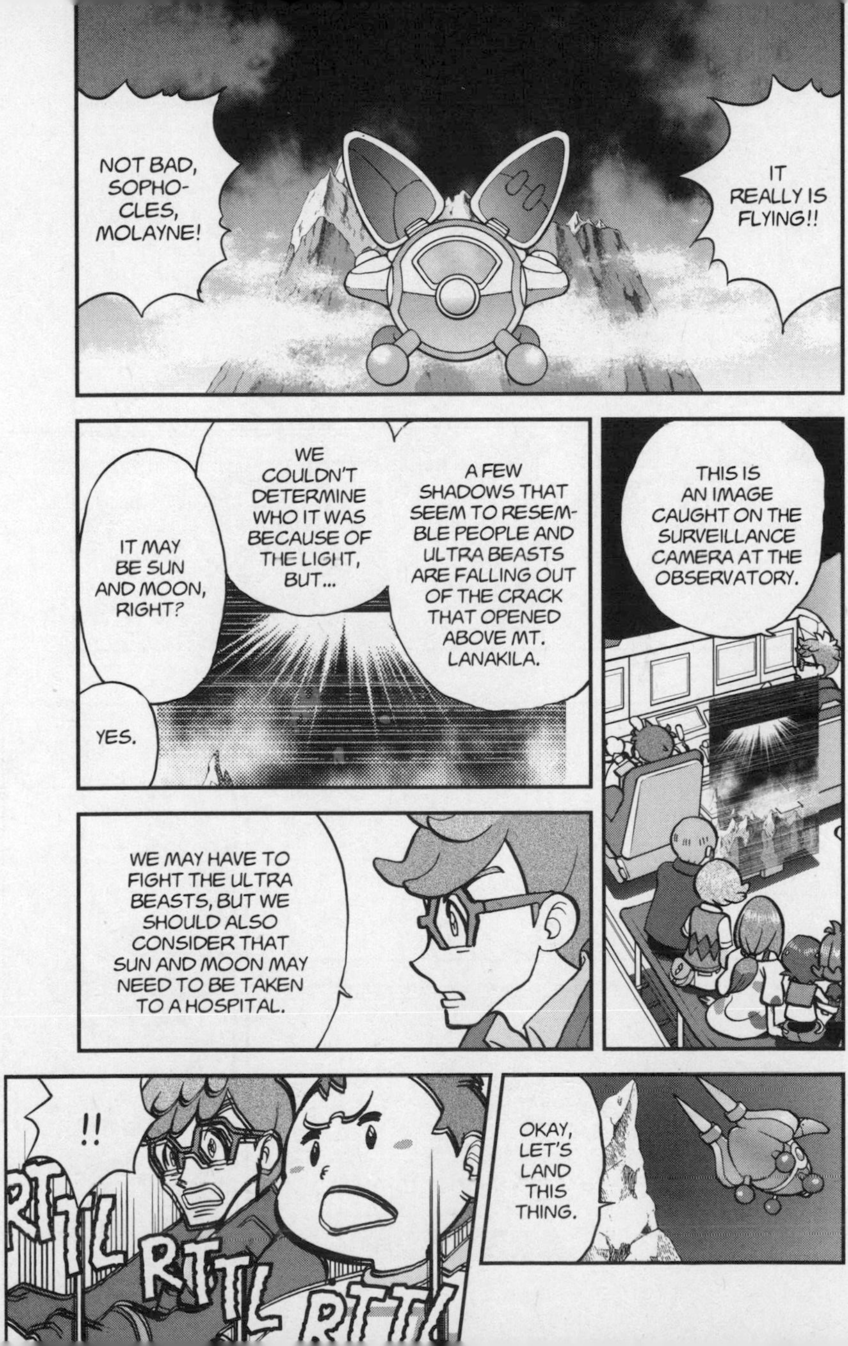
IT REALLY IS FLYING!!
NOT BAD, SOPHOCLES, MOLAYNE!
THIS IS AN IMAGE CAUGHT ON THE SURVEILLANCE CAMERA AT THE OBSERVATORY.
A FEW SHADOWS THAT SEEM TO RESEMBLE PEOPLE AND ULTRA BEASTS ARE FALLING OUT OF THE CRACK THAT OPENED ABOVE MT. LANAKILA.
WE COULDN'T DETERMINE WHO IT WAS BECAUSE OF THE LIGHT, BUT...
IT MAY BE SUN AND MOON, RIGHT?
YES.
WE MAY HAVE TO FIGHT THE ULTRA BEASTS, BUT WE SHOULD ALSO CONSIDER THAT SUN AND MOON MAY NEED TO BE TAKEN TO A HOSPITAL.
OKAY, LET'S LAND THIS THING.
!!
RTTL RTTL RTTL

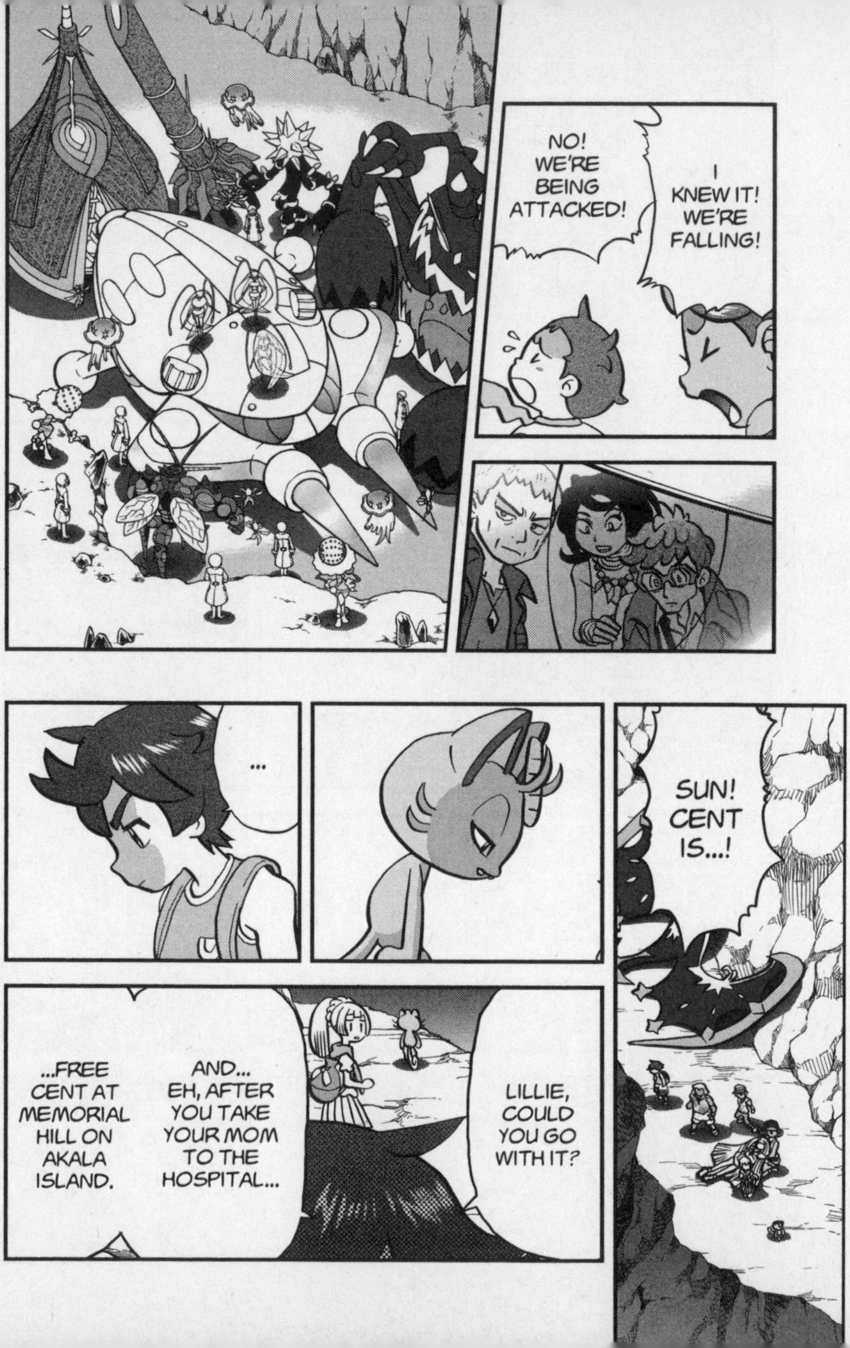
I KNEW IT! WE'RE FALLING!
NO! WE'RE BEING ATTACKED!
SUN! CENT IS...!
...
LILLIE, COULD YOU GO WITH IT?
AND... EH, AFTER YOU TAKE YOUR MOM TO THE HOSPITAL...
...FREE CENT AT MEMORIAL HILL ON AKALA ISLAND.

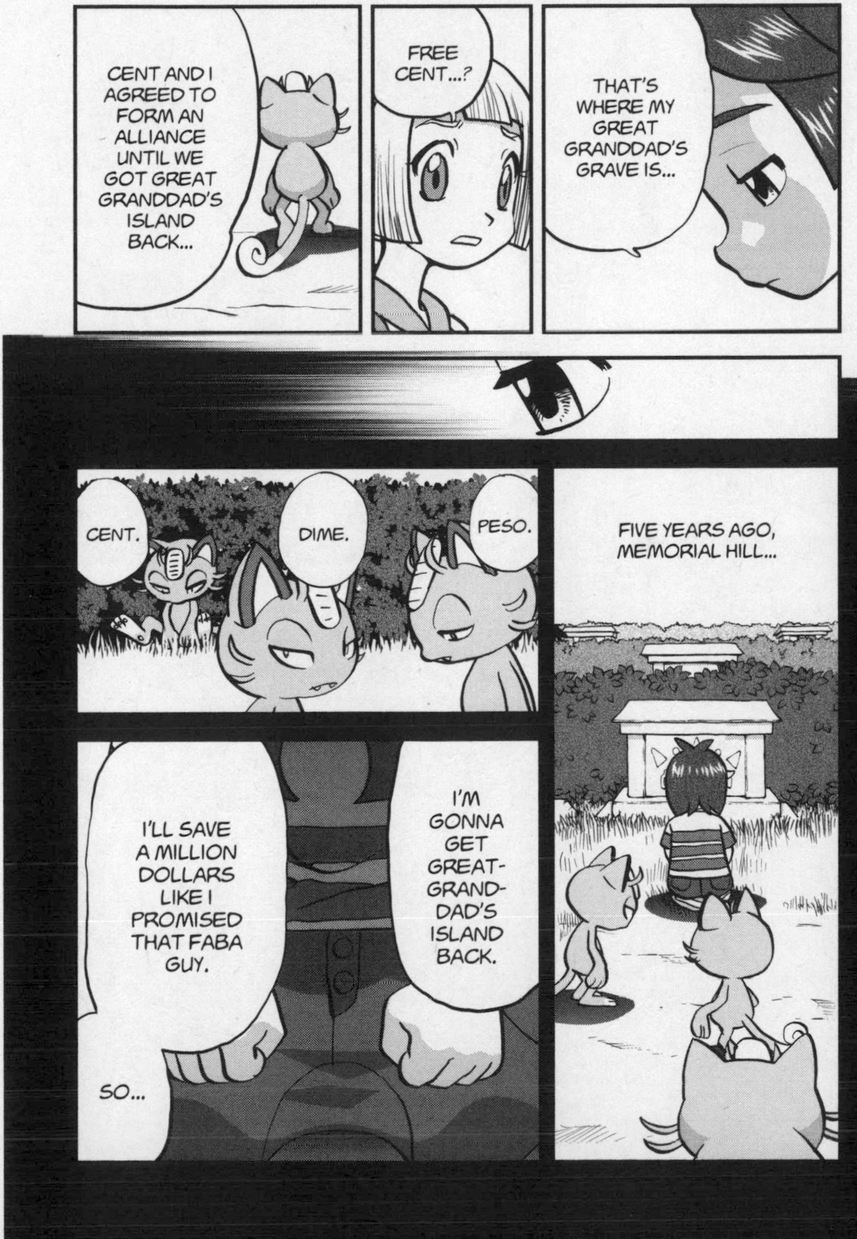
THAT'S WHERE MY GREAT GRANDDAD'S GRAVE IS...
FREE CENT...?
CENT AND I AGREED TO FORM AN ALLIANCE UNTIL WE GOT GREAT GRANDDAD'S ISLAND BACK...
FIVE YEARS AGO, MEMORIAL HILL...
PESO.
DIME.
CENT.
I'M GONNA GET GREAT-GRAND-DAD'S ISLAND BACK.
I'LL SAVE A MILLION DOLLARS LIKE I PROMISED THAT FABA GUY.
SO...

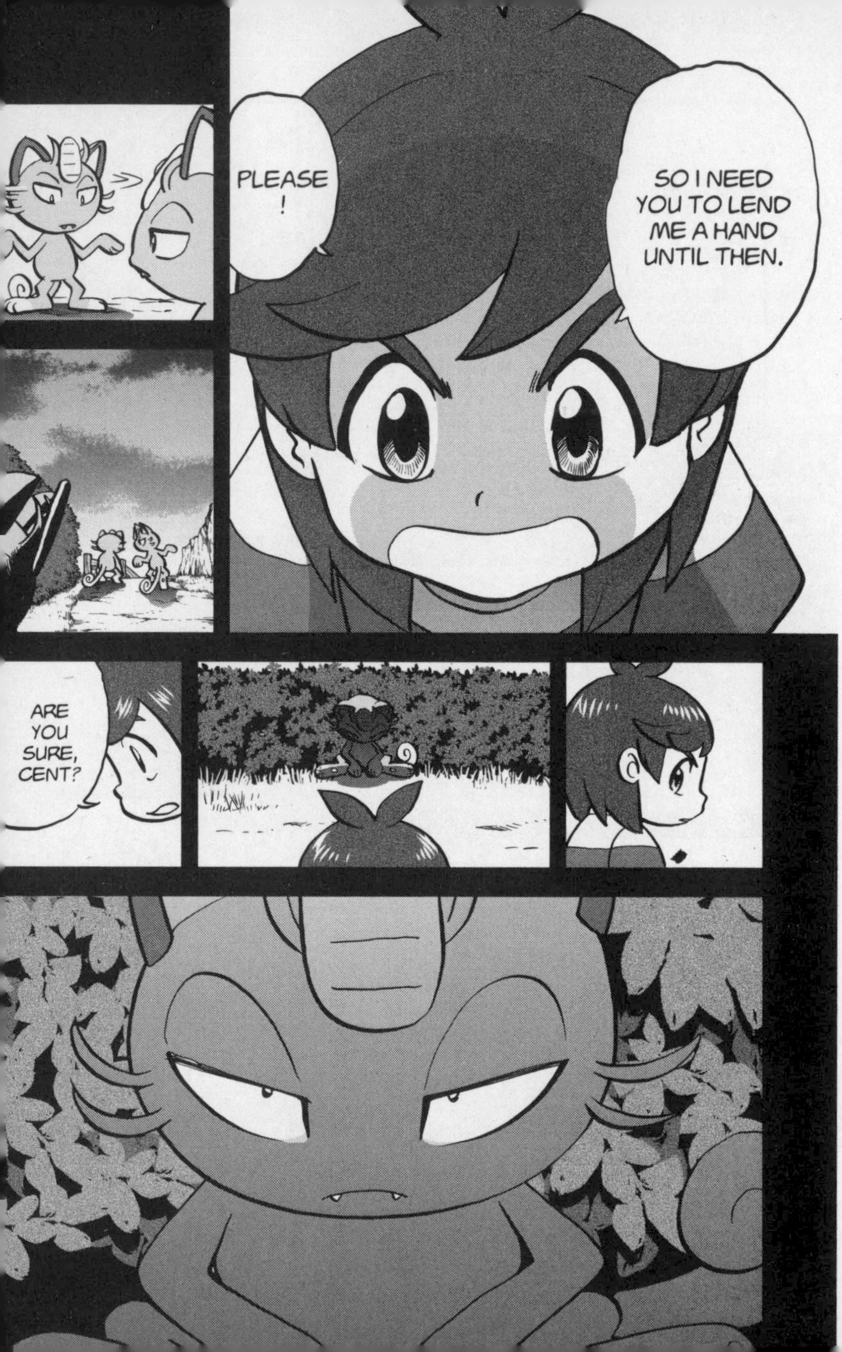
SO I NEED YOU TO LEND ME A HAND UNTIL THEN.
PLEASE!
ARE YOU SURE, CENT?

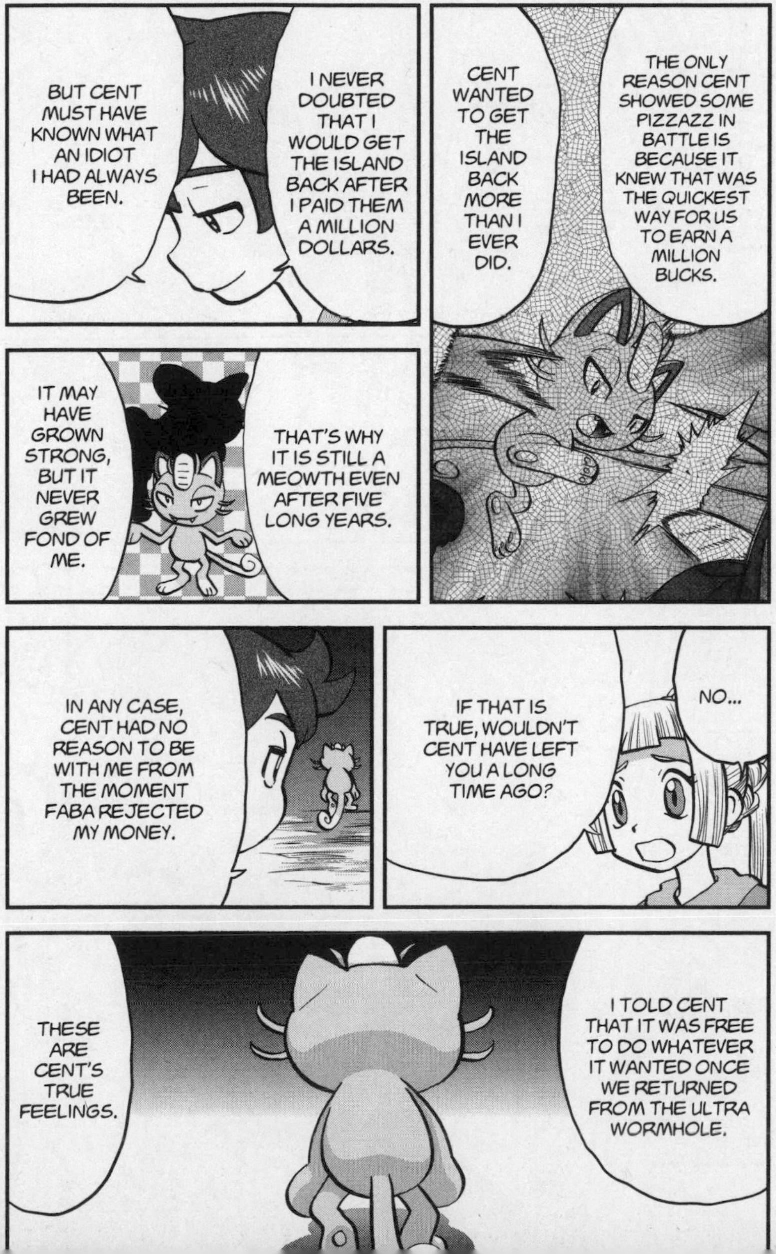
THE ONLY REASON CENT SHOWED SOME PIZZAZZ IN BATTLE IS BECAUSE IT KNEW THAT WAS THE QUICKEST WAY FOR US TO EARN A MILLION BUCKS.
CENT WANTED TO GET THE ISLAND BACK MORE THAN I EVER DID.
I NEVER DOUBTED THAT I WOULD GET THE ISLAND BACK AFTER I PAID THEM A MILLION DOLLARS.
BUT CENT MUST HAVE KNOWN WHAT AN IDIOT I HAD ALWAYS BEEN.
THAT'S WHY IT IS STILL A MEOWTH EVEN AFTER FIVE LONG YEARS.
IT MAY HAVE GROWN STRONG, BUT IT NEVER GREW FOND OF ME.
NO...
IF THAT IS TRUE, WOULDN'T CENT HAVE LEFT YOU A LONG TIME AGO?
IN ANY CASE, CENT HAD NO REASON TO BE WITH ME FROM THE MOMENT FABA REJECTED MY MONEY.
I TOLD CENT THAT IT WAS FREE TO DO WHATEVER IT WANTED ONCE WE RETURNED FROM THE ULTRA WORMHOLE.
THESE ARE CENT'S TRUE FEELINGS.

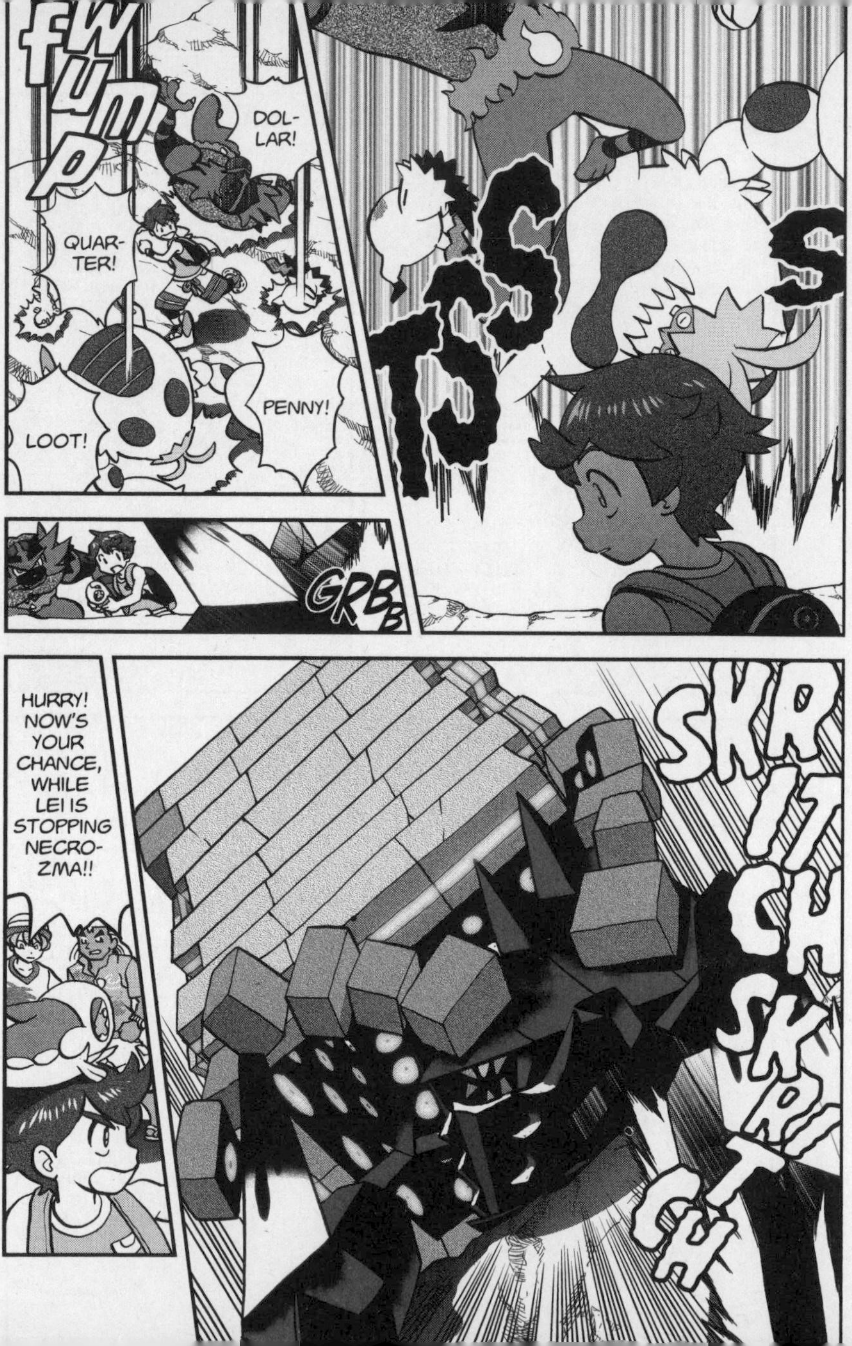
TSS
S
FWUMP
DOL-
LAR!
QUAR-
TER!
PENNY!
LOOT!
GRBB
SKRITCH
SKRITCH
HURRY! NOW'S YOUR CHANCE, WHILE LEI IS STOPPING NECRO-
ZMA!!

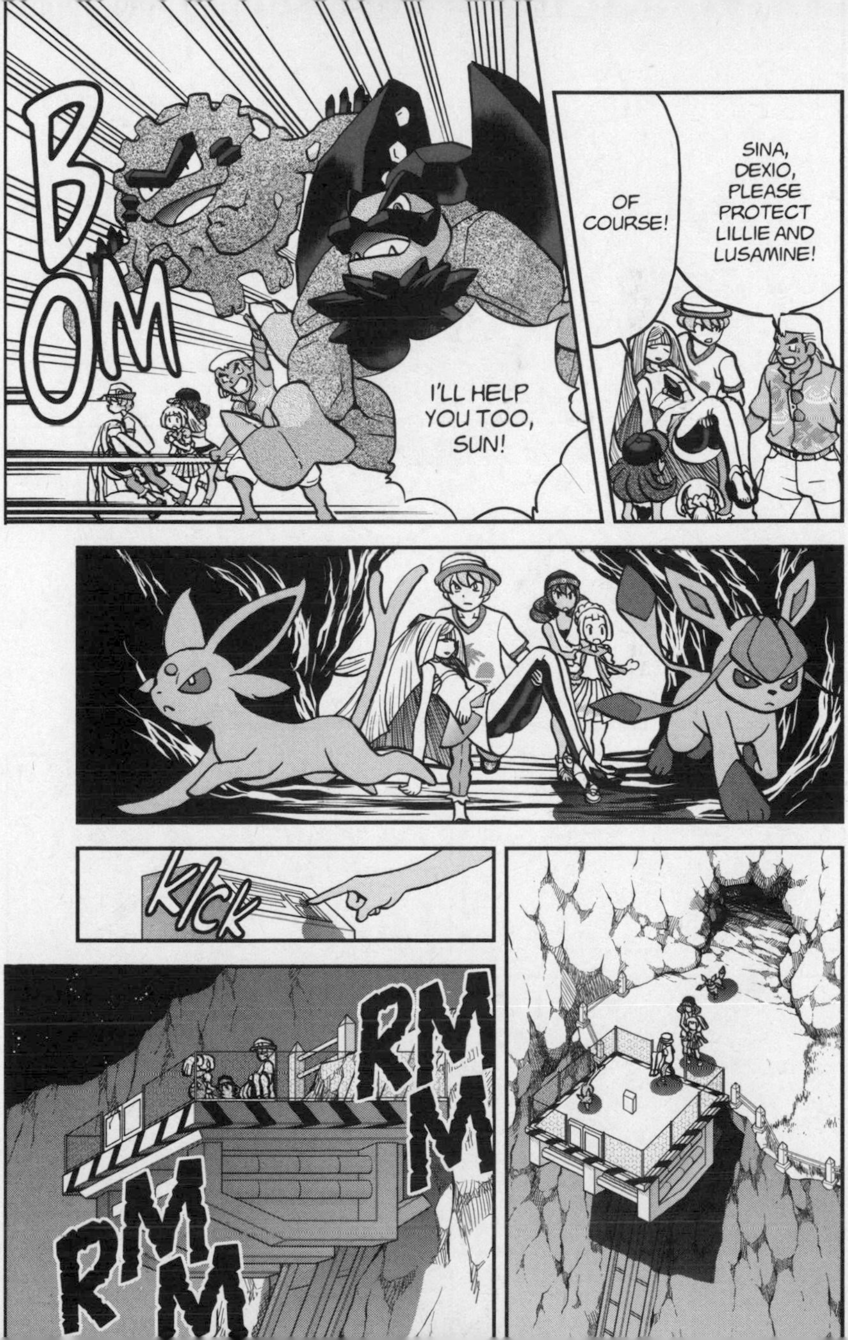
SINA, DEXIO, PLEASE PROTECT LILLIE AND LUSAMINE!
OF COURSE!
B OM
I'LL HELP YOU TOO, SUN!
KLICK
RMM
RMM

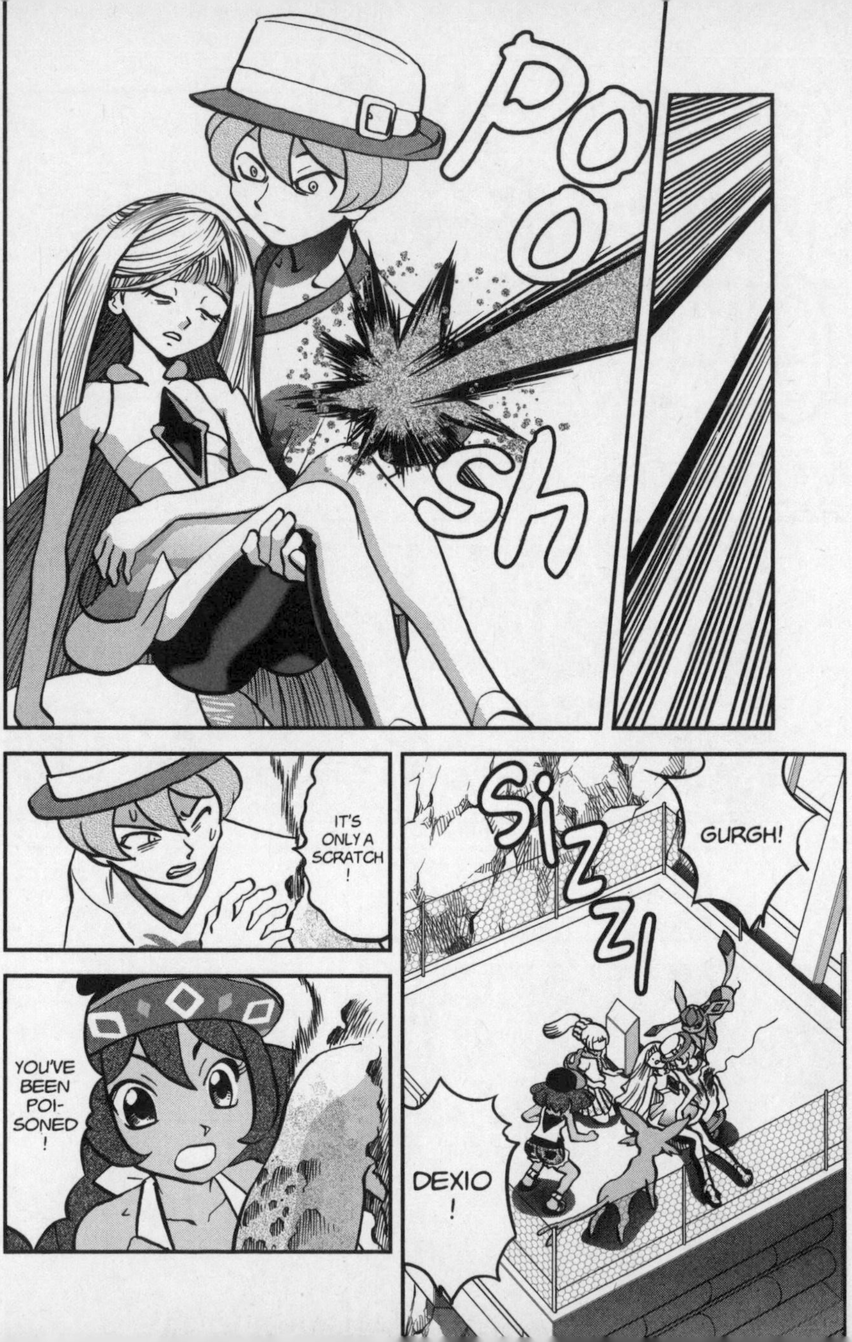
POOOSH
GURGH!
SIZZZL
DEXIO!
IT'S ONLY A SCRATCH!
YOU'VE BEEN POI-SONED!

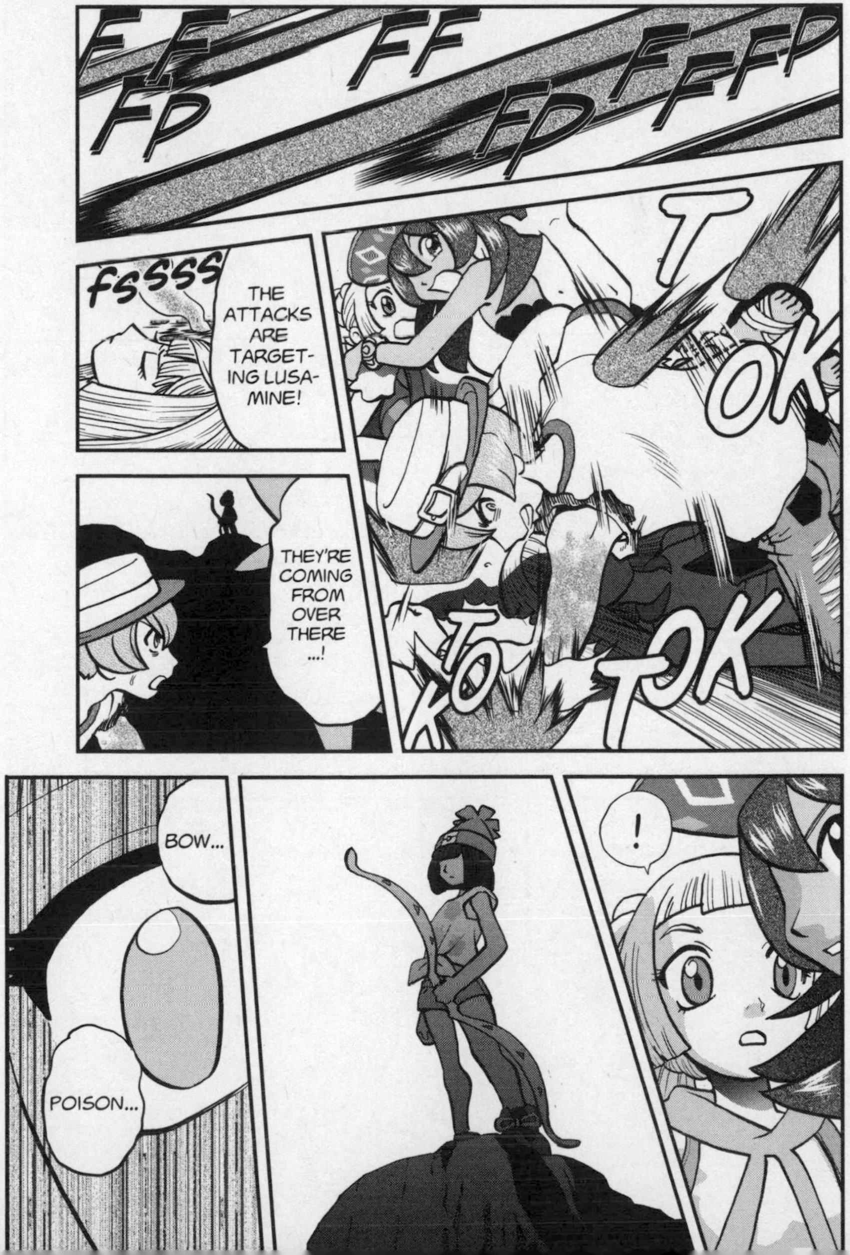
FFFP
FF
FFFFP
FP
TOK
TOK
TOK
fsssss
THE ATTACKS ARE TARGET-ING LUSA-MINE!
THEY'RE COMING FROM OVER THERE ...!
!
BOW...
POISON...

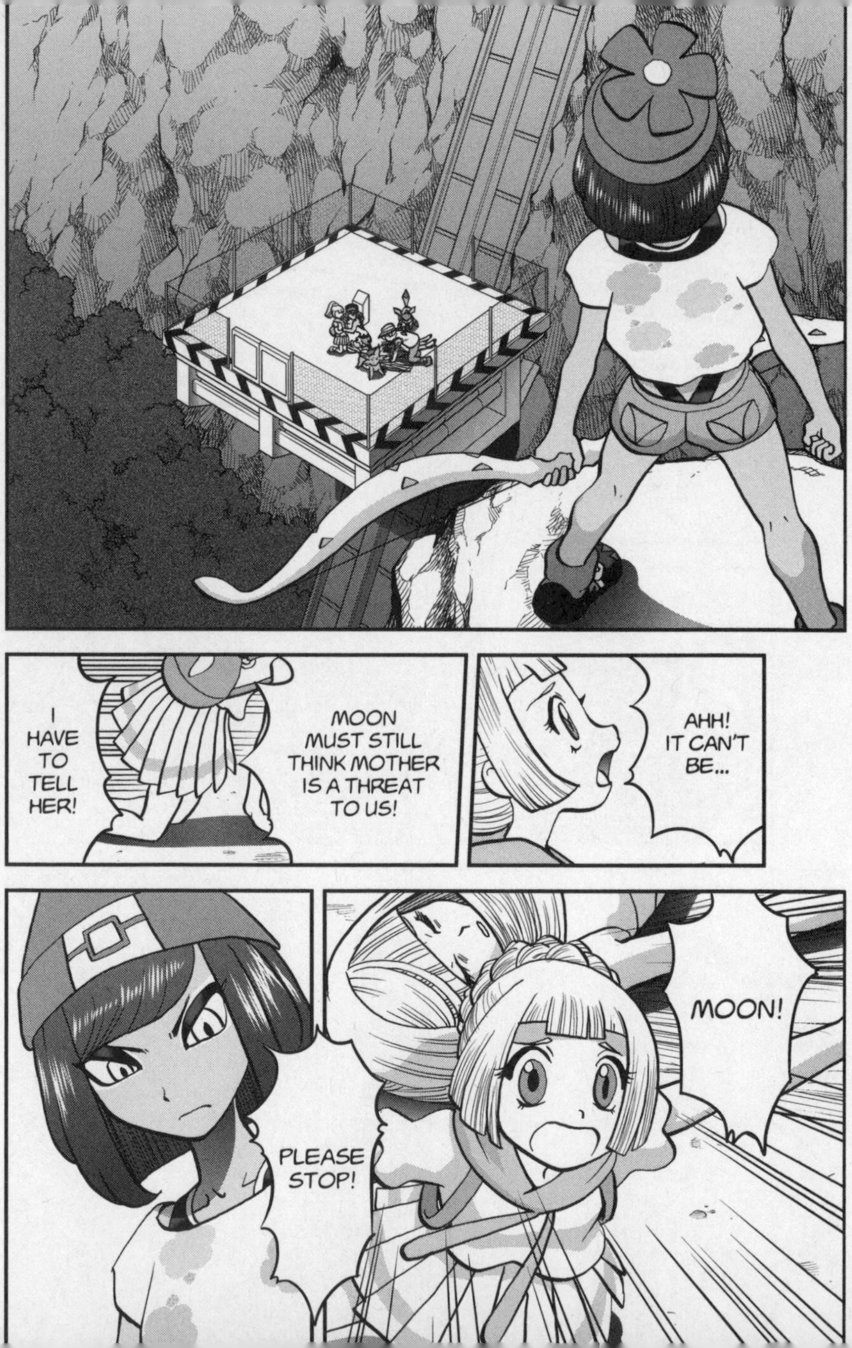
AHH! IT CAN'T BE...
MOON MUST STILL THINK MOTHER IS A THREAT TO US!
I HAVE TO TELL HER!
MOON!
PLEASE STOP!

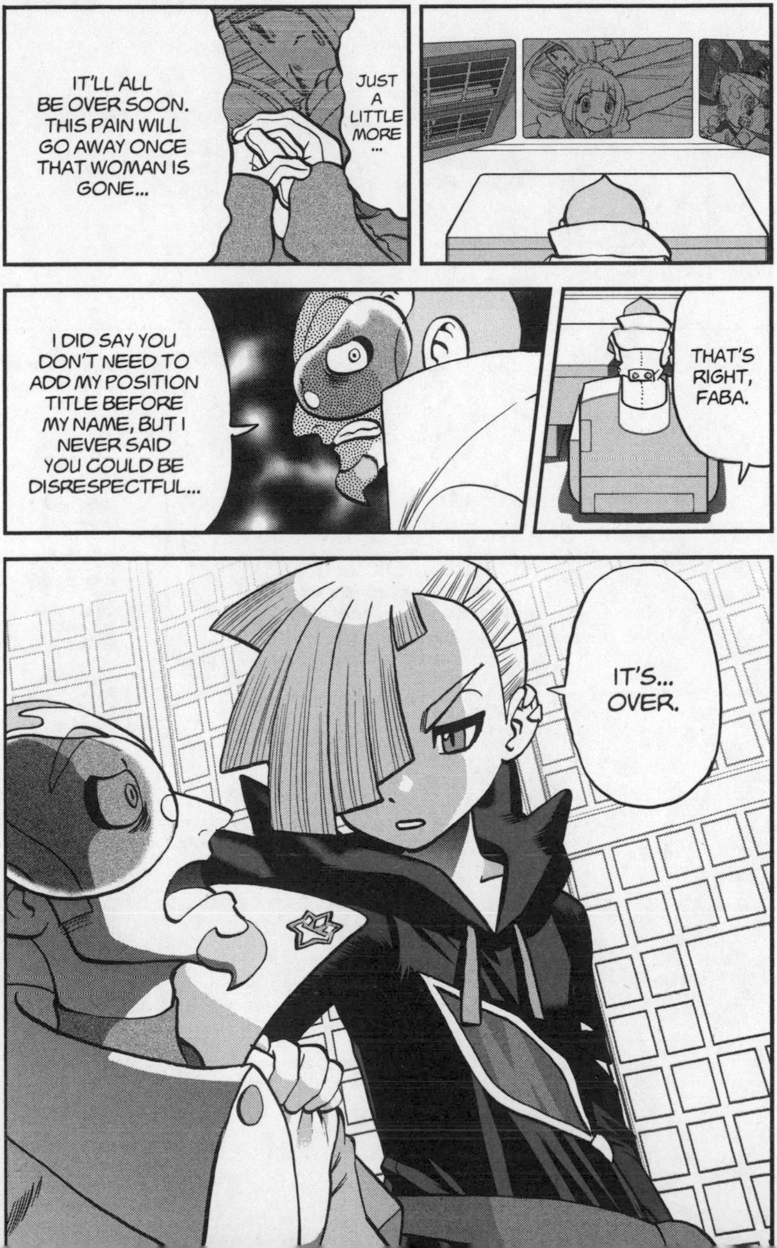
JUST A LITTLE MORE...
IT'LL ALL BE OVER SOON. THIS PAIN WILL GO AWAY ONCE THAT WOMAN IS GONE...
THAT'S RIGHT, FABA.
I DID SAY YOU DON'T NEED TO ADD MY POSITION TITLE BEFORE MY NAME, BUT I NEVER SAID YOU COULD BE DISRESPECTFUL...
IT'S... OVER.

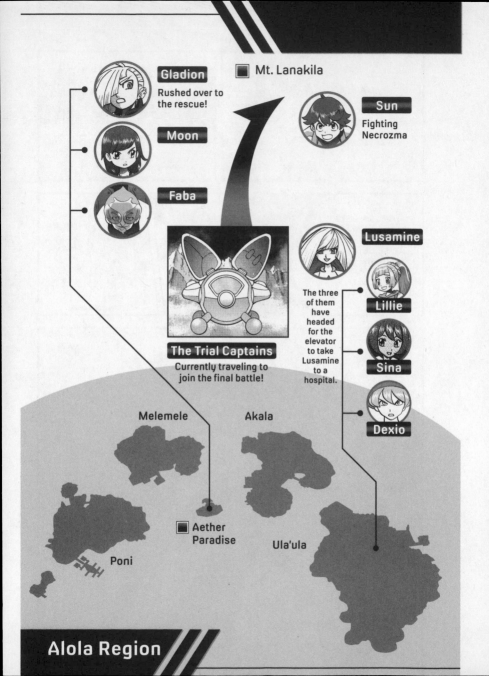

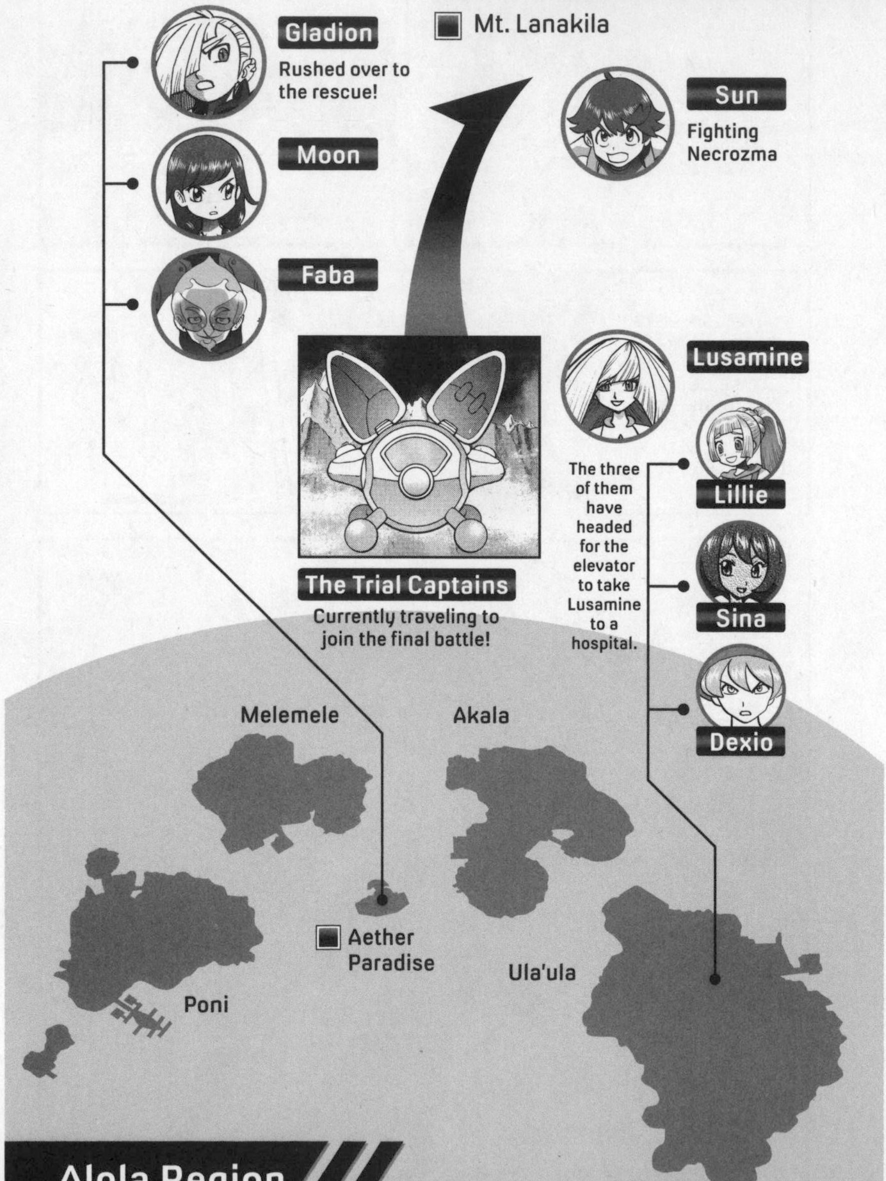
Mt. Lanakila
Gladion
Rushed over to the rescue!
Moon
Faba
Sun
Fighting Necrozma
Lusamine
The three of them have headed for the elevator to take Lusamine to a hospital.
Lillie
Sina
Dexio
The Trial Captains
Currently traveling to join the final battle!
Melemele
Akala
Aether Paradise
Ula'ula
Poni

Alola Region

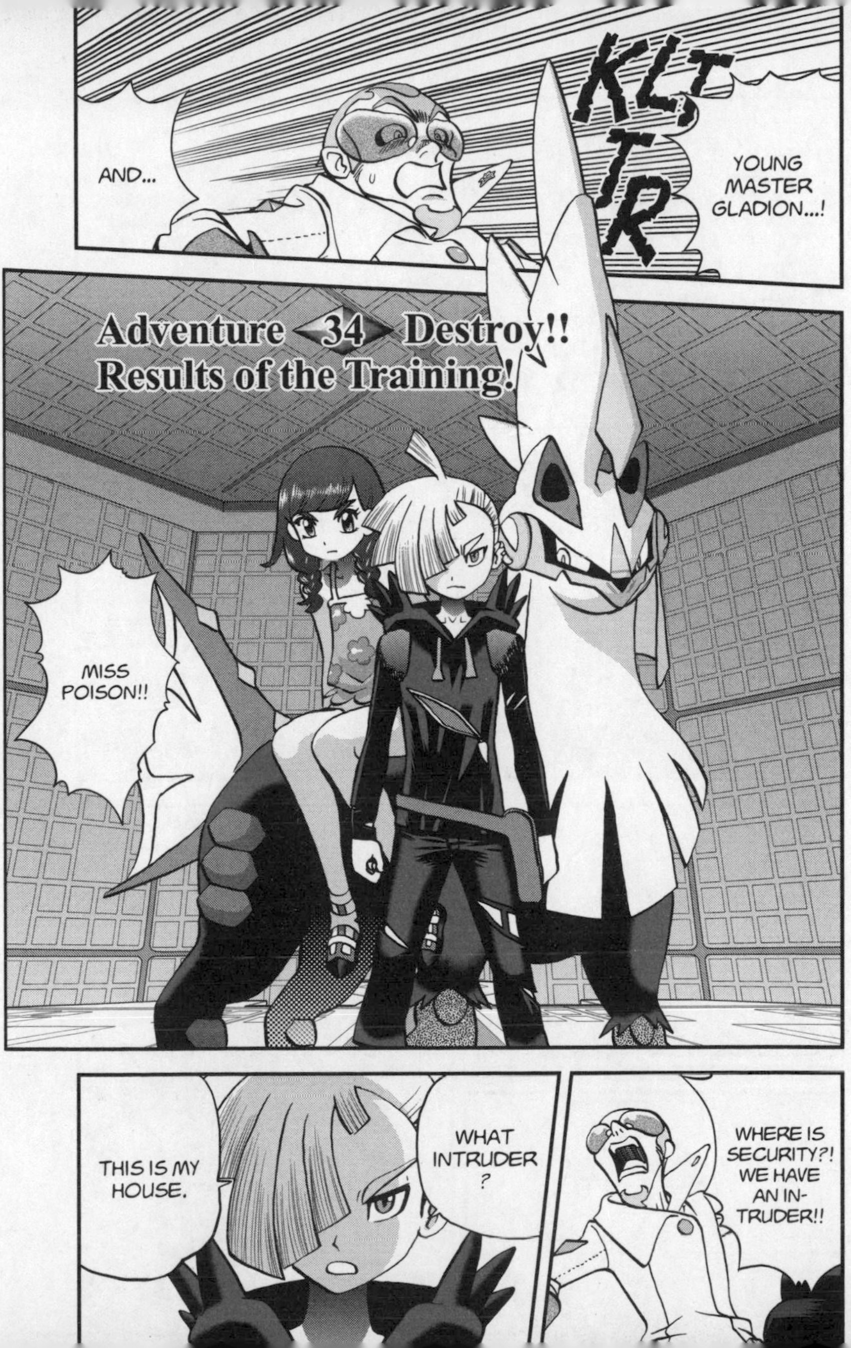
YOUNG MASTER GLADION...!
KLTTR
AND...
Adventure 34 Destroy!! Results of the Training!
MISS POISON!!
WHERE IS SECURITY?! WE HAVE AN INTRUDER!!
WHAT INTRUDER?
THIS IS MY HOUSE.

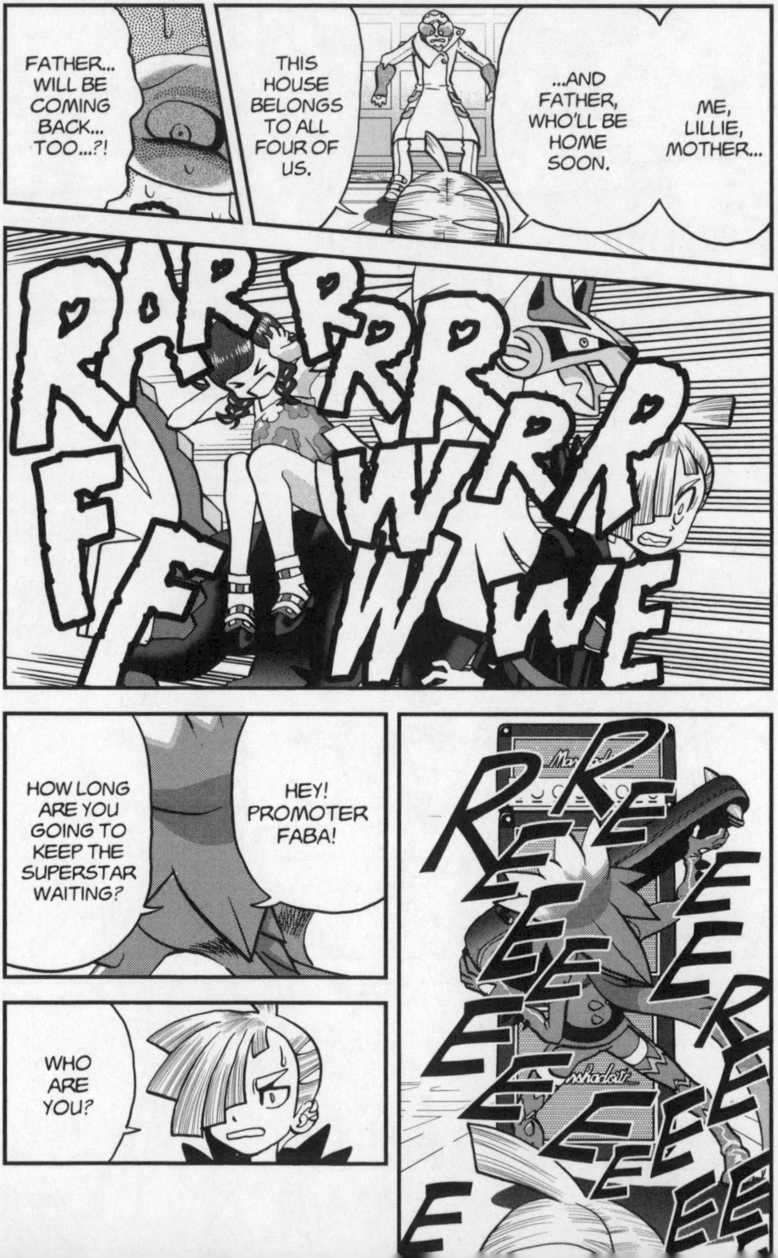
ME, LILLIE, MOTHER...
...AND FATHER, WHO'LL BE HOME SOON.
THIS HOUSE BELONGS TO ALL FOUR OF US.
FATHER... WILL BE COMING BACK... TOO...?!
HEY! PROMOTER FABA!
HOW LONG ARE YOU GOING TO KEEP THE SUPERSTAR WAITING?
WHO ARE YOU?

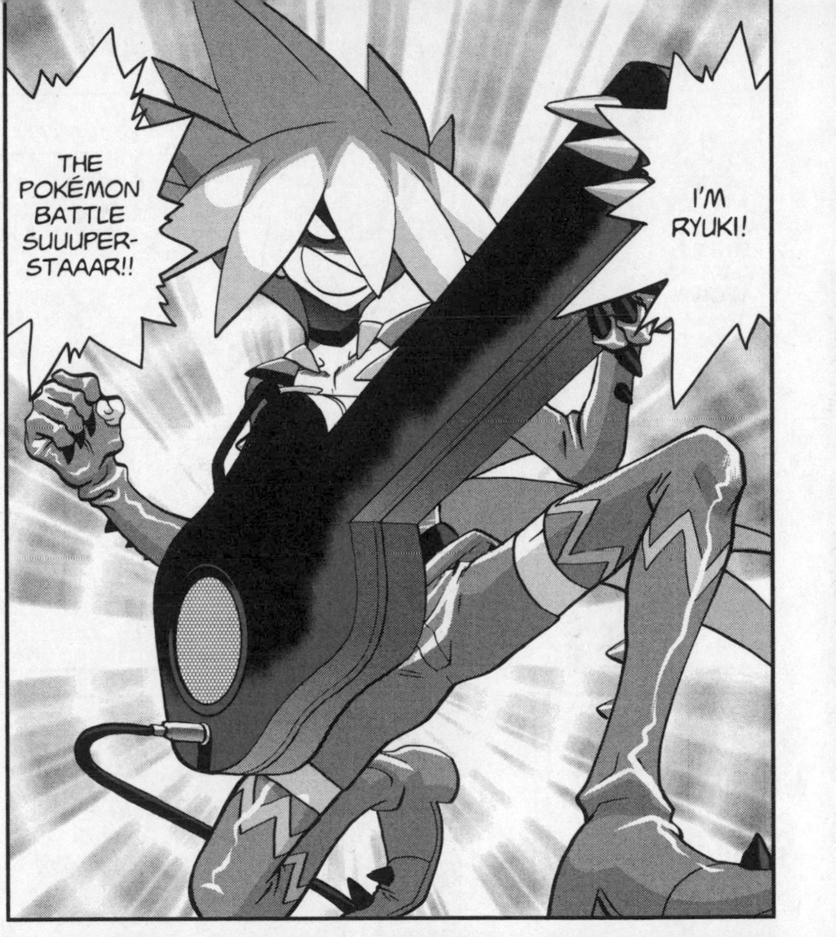
I'M RYUKI!
THE POKÉMON BATTLE SUUUPER-STAAAR!!

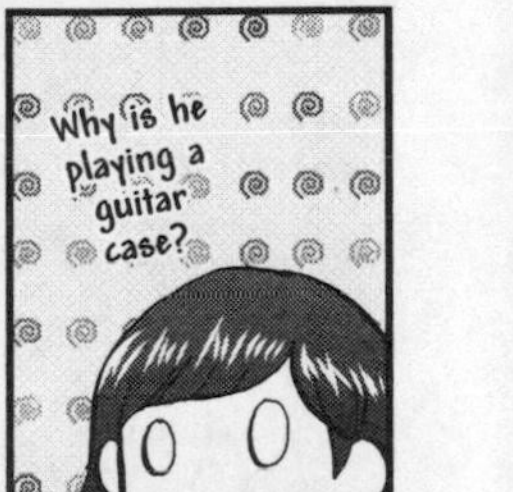
Why is he playing a guitar case?

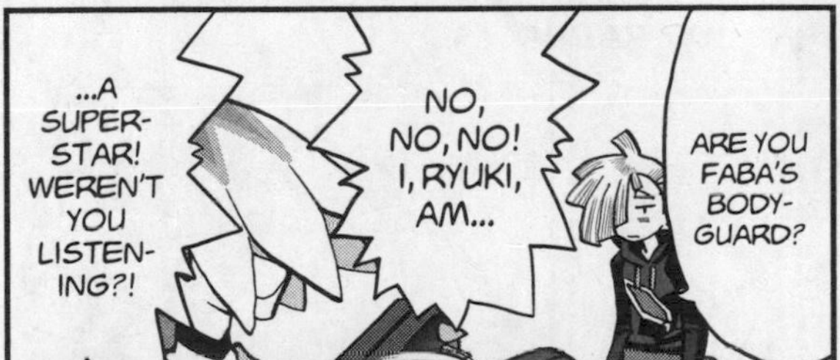
ARE YOU FABA'S BODY-GUARD?
NO, NO, NO! I, RYUKI, AM...
...A SUPER-STAR! WEREN'T YOU LISTEN-ING?!

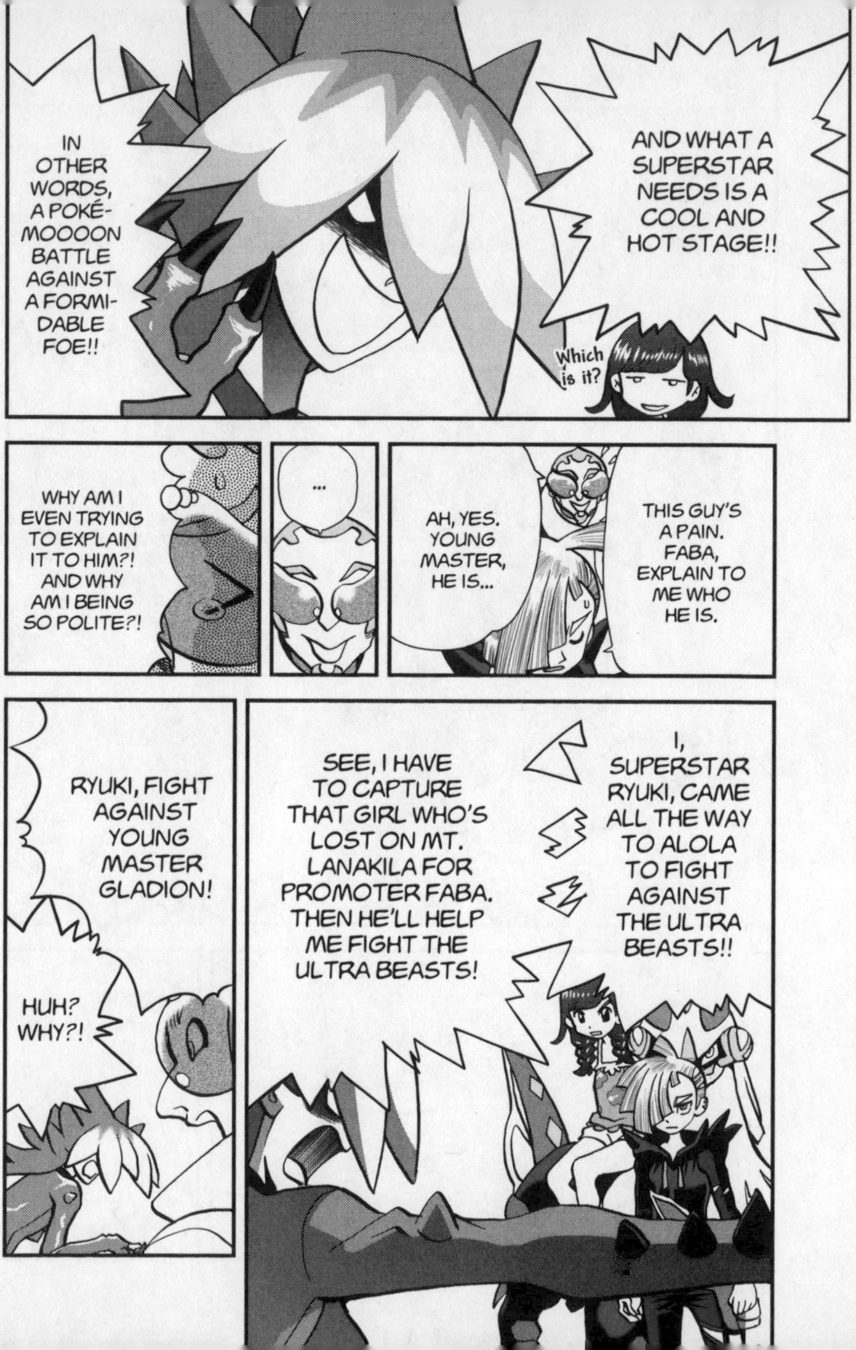
AND WHAT A SUPERSTAR NEEDS IS A COOL AND HOT STAGE!!
IN OTHER WORDS, A POKÉ-MOOOON BATTLE AGAINST A FORMIDABLE FOE!!
Which is it?
THIS GUY'S A PAIN. FABA, EXPLAIN TO ME WHO HE IS.
AH, YES. YOUNG MASTER, HE IS...
...
WHY AM I EVEN TRYING TO EXPLAIN IT TO HIM?! AND WHY AM I BEING SO POLITE?!
I, SUPERSTAR RYUKI, CAME ALL THE WAY TO ALOLA TO FIGHT AGAINST THE ULTRA BEASTS!!
SEE, I HAVE TO CAPTURE THAT GIRL WHO'S LOST ON MT. LANAKILA FOR PROMOTER FABA. THEN HE'LL HELP ME FIGHT THE ULTRA BEASTS!
RYUKI, FIGHT AGAINST YOUNG MASTER GLADION!
HUH? WHY?!

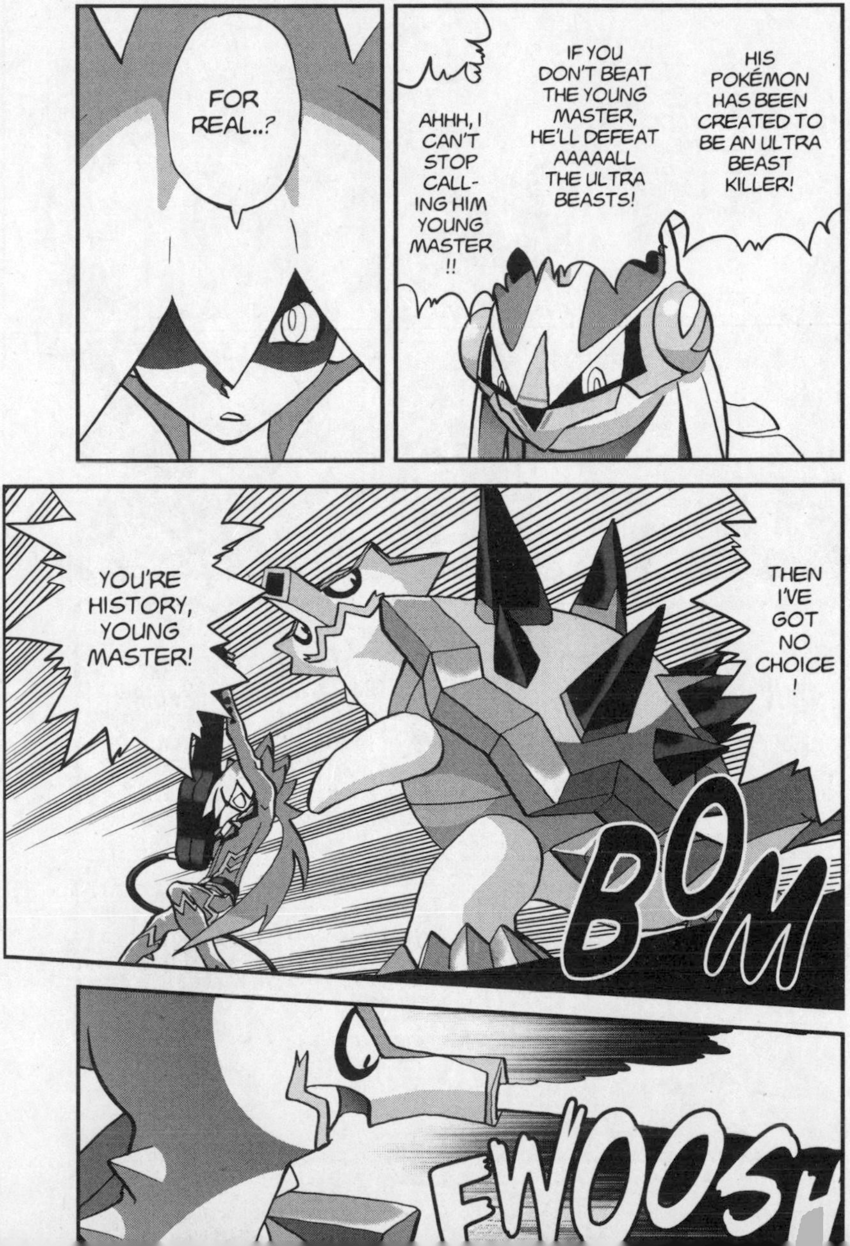
HIS POKÉMON HAS BEEN CREATED TO BE AN ULTRA BEAST KILLER!
IF YOU DON'T BEAT THE YOUNG MASTER, HE'LL DEFEAT AAAAALL THE ULTRA BEASTS!
AHHH, I CAN'T STOP CALL-ING HIM YOUNG MASTER!!
FOR REAL..?
THEN I'VE GOT NO CHOICE!
YOU'RE HISTORY, YOUNG MASTER!
BOOM
FWOOSH

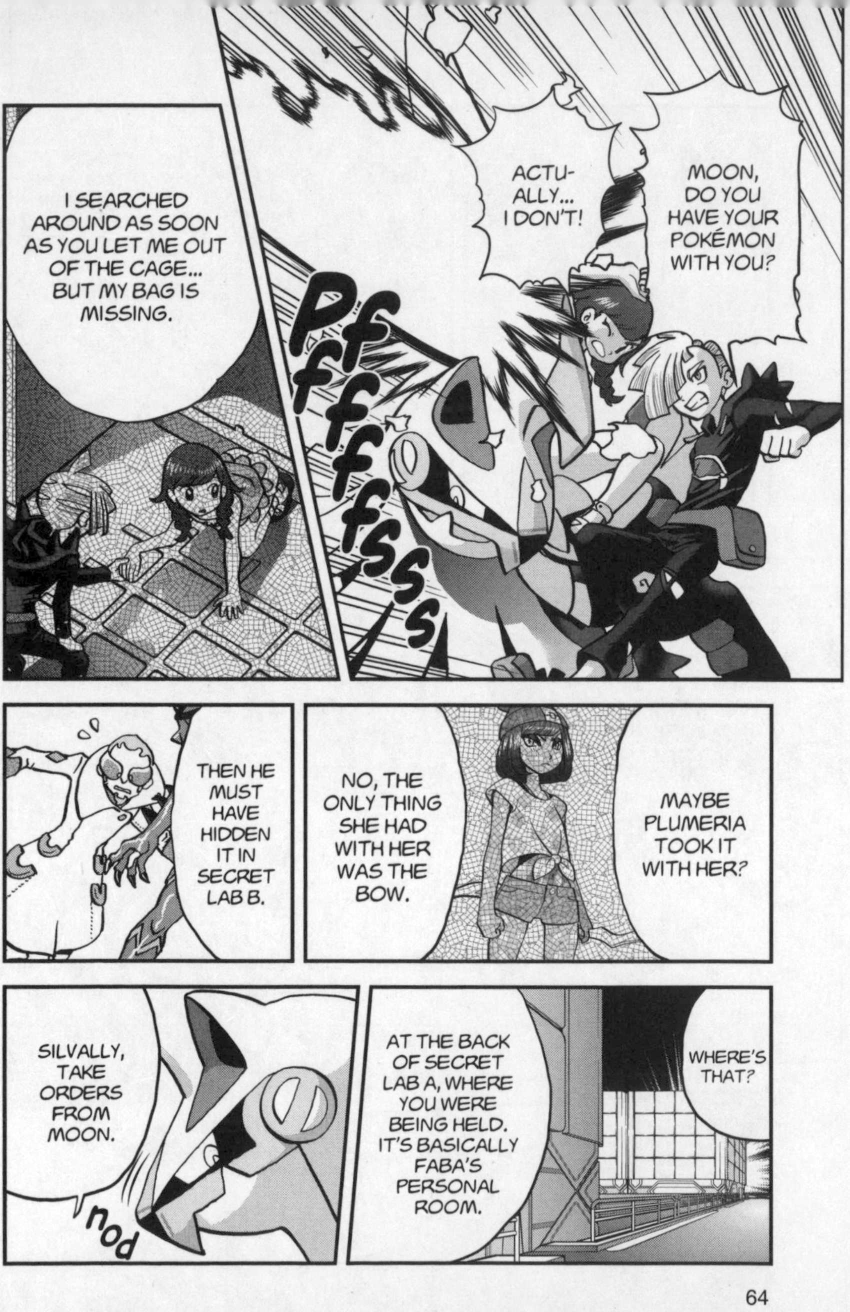
MOON, DO YOU HAVE YOUR POKÉMON WITH YOU?
ACTU-ALLY... I DON'T!
Pffffffssss
I SEARCHED AROUND AS SOON AS YOU LET ME OUT OF THE CAGE... BUT MY BAG IS MISSING.
MAYBE PLUMERIA TOOK IT WITH HER?
NO, THE ONLY THING SHE HAD WITH HER WAS THE BOW.
THEN HE MUST HAVE HIDDEN IT IN SECRET LAB B.
WHERE'S THAT?
AT THE BACK OF SECRET LAB A, WHERE YOU WERE BEING HELD. IT'S BASICALLY FABA'S PERSONAL ROOM.
SILVALLY, TAKE ORDERS FROM MOON.
nod

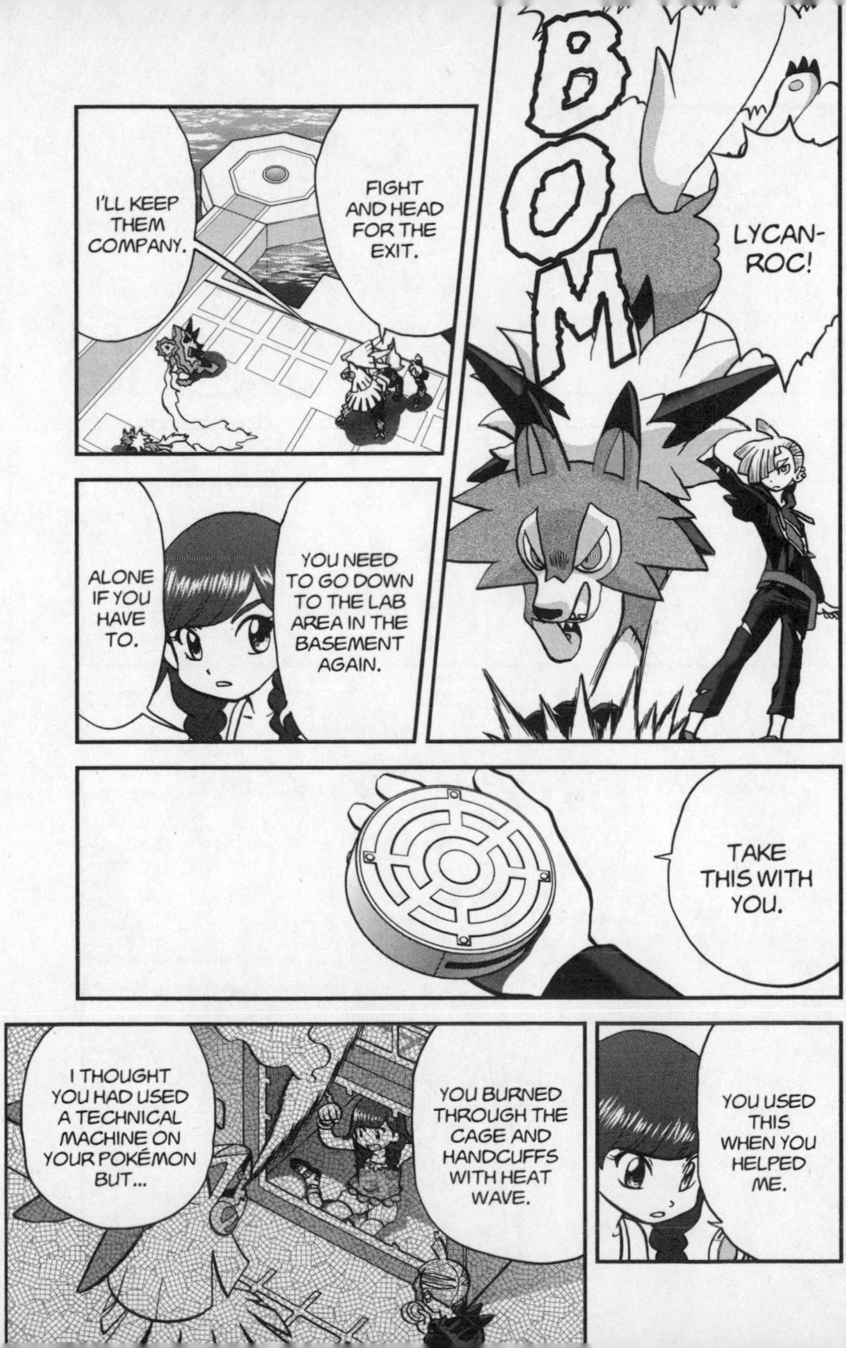
BOOM
LYCAN-ROC!
FIGHT AND HEAD FOR THE EXIT.
I'LL KEEP THEM COMPANY.
YOU NEED TO GO DOWN TO THE LAB AREA IN THE BASEMENT AGAIN.
ALONE IF YOU HAVE TO.
TAKE THIS WITH YOU.
YOU USED THIS WHEN YOU HELPED ME.
YOU BURNED THROUGH THE CAGE AND HANDCUFFS WITH HEAT WAVE.
I THOUGHT YOU HAD USED A TECHNICAL MACHINE ON YOUR POKÉMON BUT...

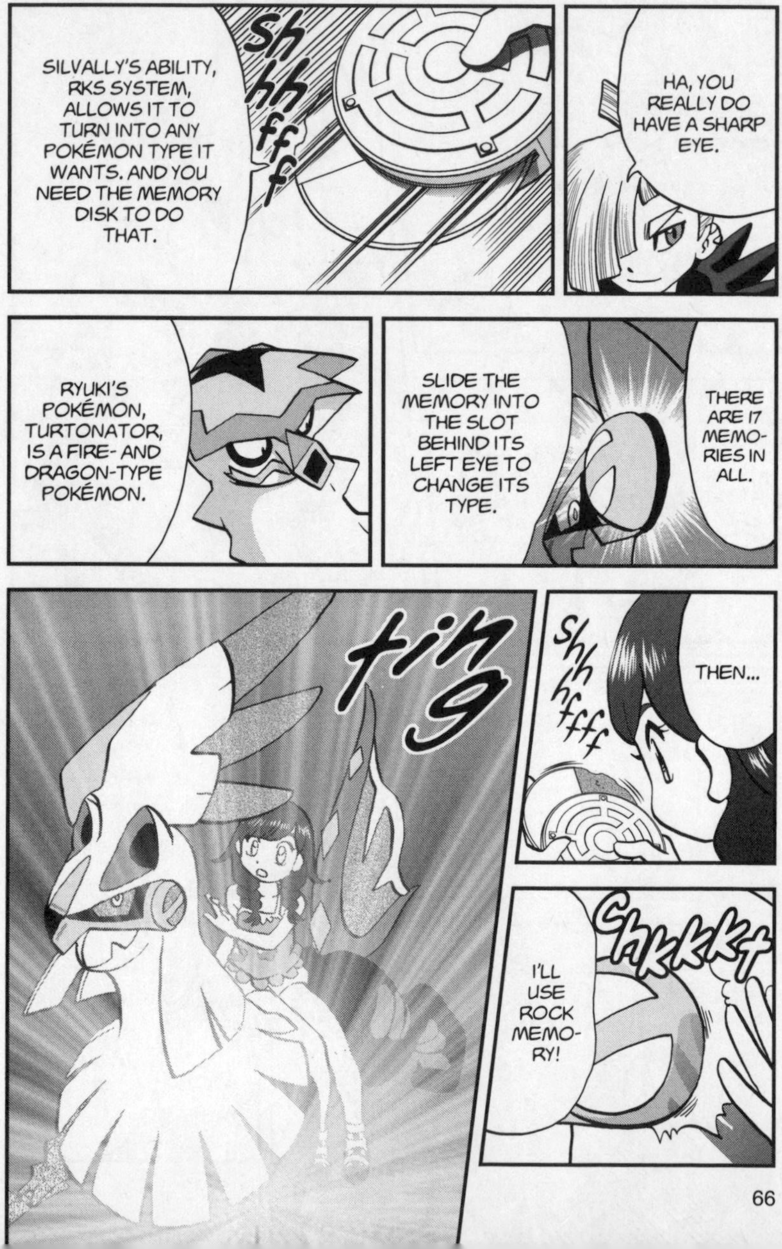
HA, YOU REALLY DO HAVE A SHARP EYE.
SILVALLY'S ABILITY, RKS SYSTEM, ALLOWS IT TO TURN INTO ANY POKÉMON TYPE IT WANTS. AND YOU NEED THE MEMORY DISK TO DO THAT.
shhhfff
THERE ARE 17 MEMORIES IN ALL.
SLIDE THE MEMORY INTO THE SLOT BEHIND ITS LEFT EYE TO CHANGE ITS TYPE.
RYUKI'S POKÉMON, TURTONATOR, IS A FIRE- AND DRAGON-TYPE POKÉMON.
shhhhffff
THEN...
chkkkt
I'LL USE ROCK MEMORY!
ting

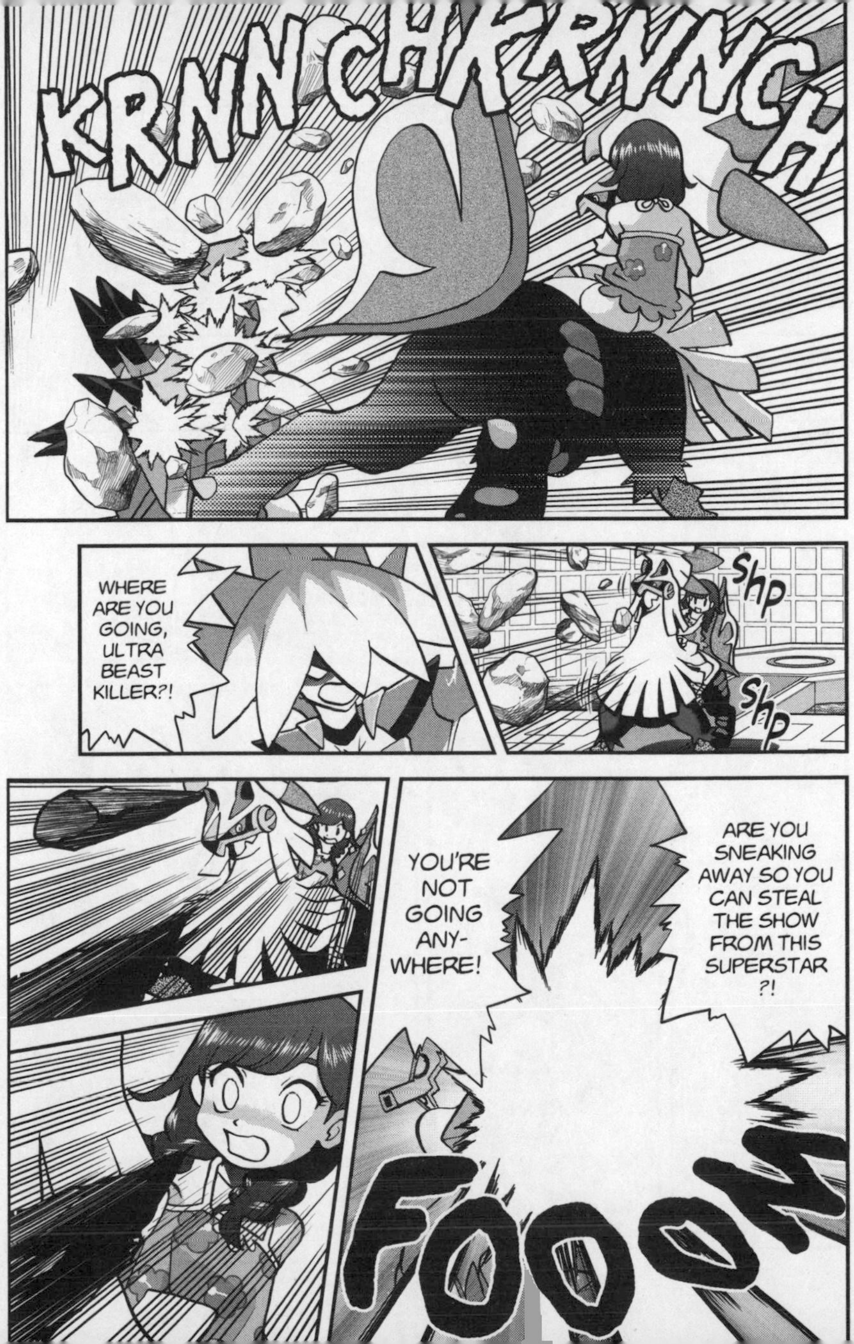
KRNNCHKRNNCH
Shp
Shp
WHERE ARE YOU GOING, ULTRA BEAST KILLER?!
ARE YOU SNEAKING AWAY SO YOU CAN STEAL THE SHOW FROM THIS SUPERSTAR?!
YOU'RE NOT GOING ANY-WHERE!
FOOOM

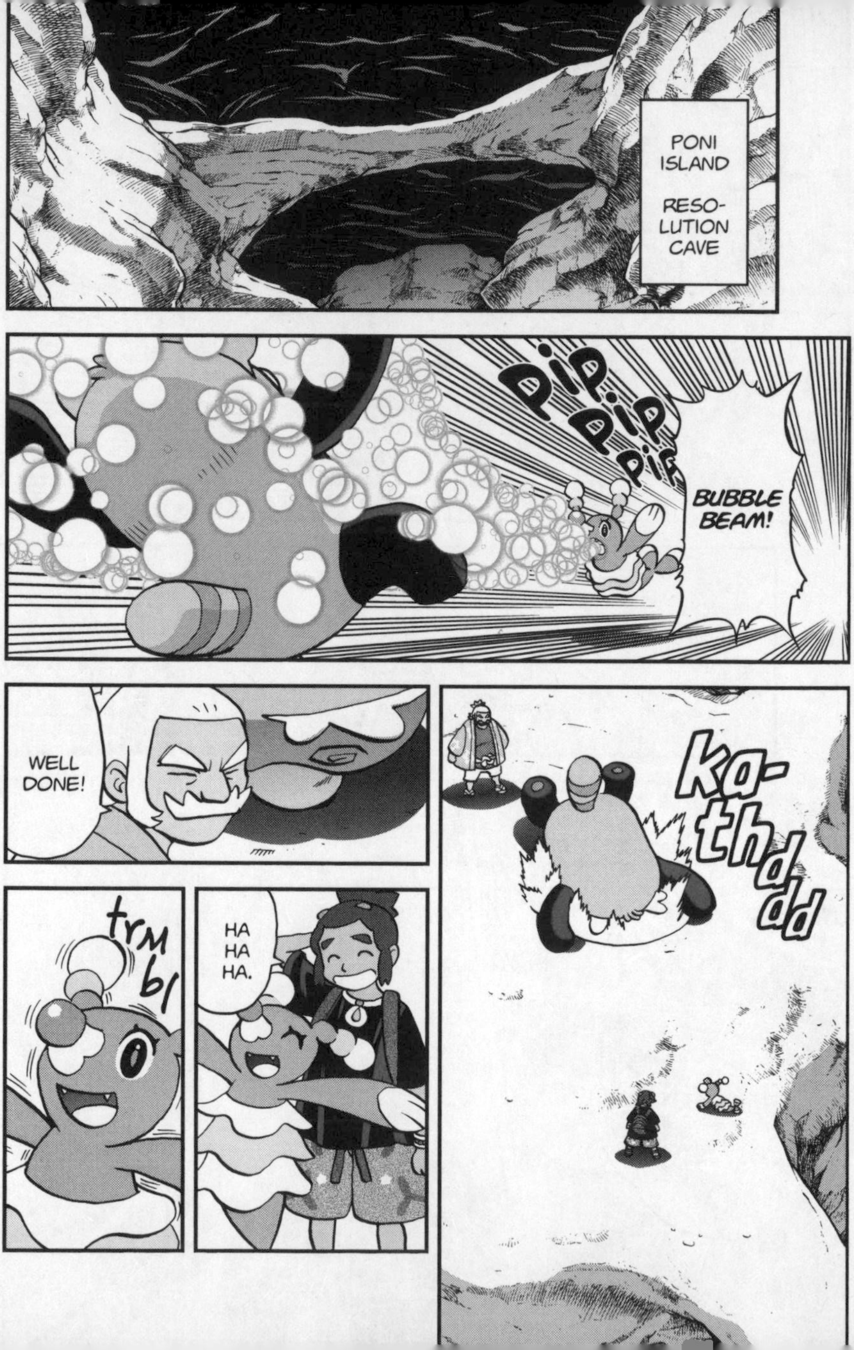
PONI ISLAND
RESO-
LUTION
CAVE
PIP PIP PIP
BUBBLE BEAM!
ka-thddd
WELL DONE!
HA HA HA.
trmbl

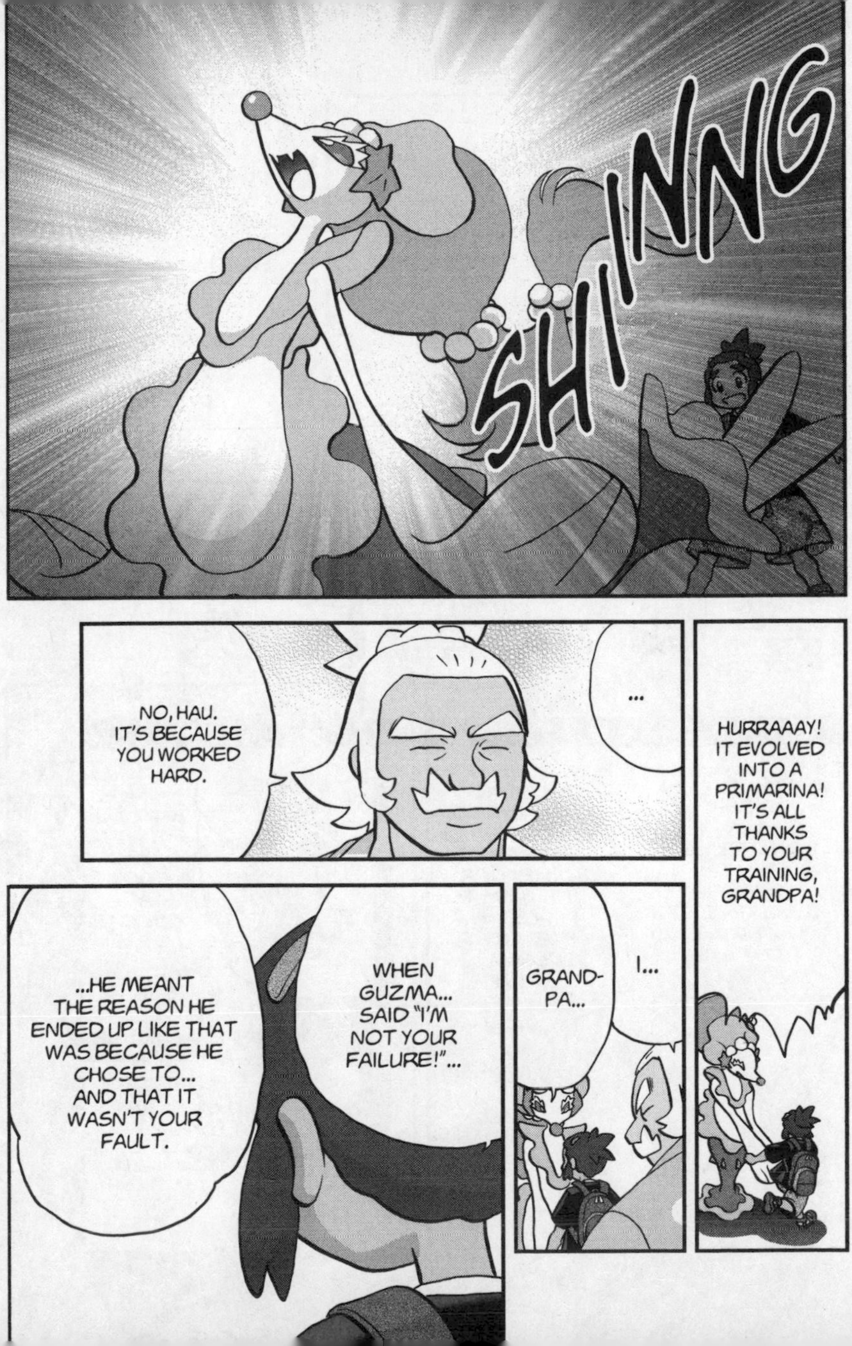
SHIINNG
HURRAAAY! IT EVOLVED INTO A PRIMARINA! IT'S ALL THANKS TO YOUR TRAINING, GRANDPA!
...
NO, HAU. IT'S BECAUSE YOU WORKED HARD.
I...
GRAND-PA...
WHEN GUZMA... SAID "I'M NOT YOUR FAILURE!"...
...HE MEANT THE REASON HE ENDED UP LIKE THAT WAS BECAUSE HE CHOSE TO... AND THAT IT WASN'T YOUR FAULT.

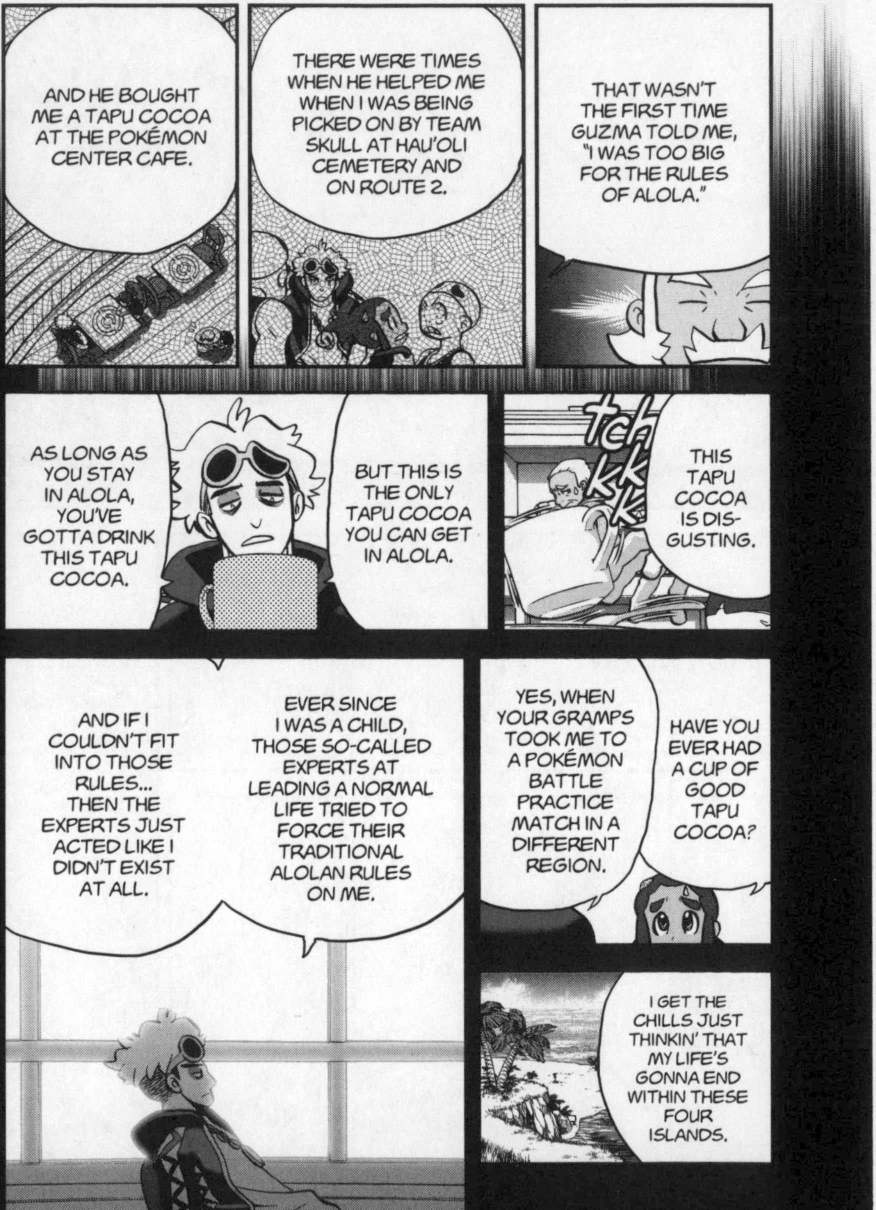
THAT WASN'T THE FIRST TIME GUZMA TOLD ME, "I WAS TOO BIG FOR THE RULES OF ALOLA."
THERE WERE TIMES WHEN HE HELPED ME WHEN I WAS BEING PICKED ON BY TEAM SKULL AT HAU'OLI CEMETERY AND ON ROUTE 2.
AND HE BOUGHT ME A TAPU COCOA AT THE POKÉMON CENTER CAFE.
tchkkk
THIS TAPU COCOA IS DIS-GUSTING.
BUT THIS IS THE ONLY TAPU COCOA YOU CAN GET IN ALOLA.
AS LONG AS YOU STAY IN ALOLA, YOU'VE GOTTA DRINK THIS TAPU COCOA.
HAVE YOU EVER HAD A CUP OF GOOD TAPU COCOA?
YES, WHEN YOUR GRAMPS TOOK ME TO A POKÉMON BATTLE PRACTICE MATCH IN A DIFFERENT REGION.
I GET THE CHILLS JUST THINKIN' THAT MY LIFE'S GONNA END WITHIN THESE FOUR ISLANDS.
EVER SINCE I WAS A CHILD, THOSE SO-CALLED EXPERTS AT LEADING A NORMAL LIFE TRIED TO FORCE THEIR TRADITIONAL ALOLAN RULES ON ME.
AND IF I COULDN'T FIT INTO THOSE RULES... THEN THE EXPERTS JUST ACTED LIKE I DIDN'T EXIST AT ALL.

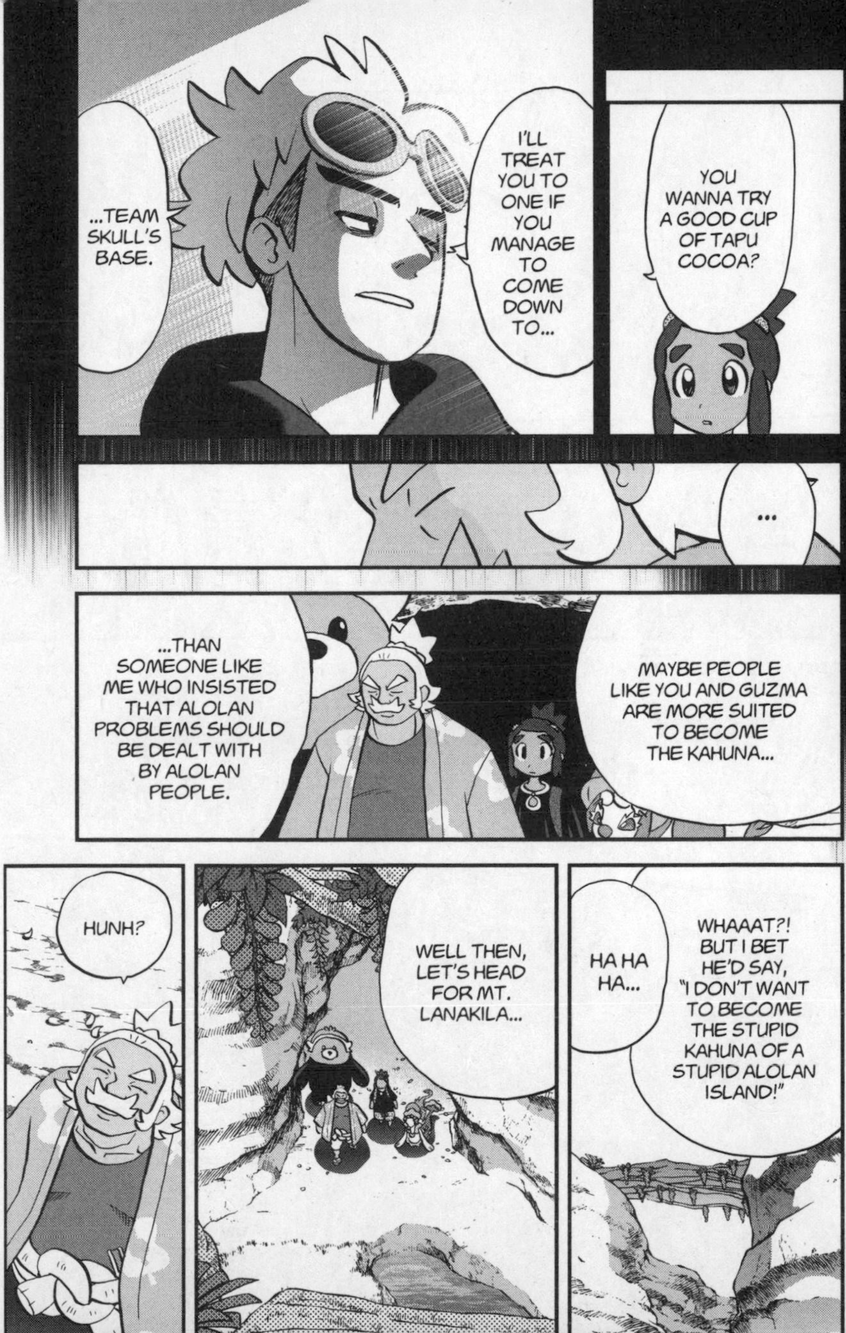
YOU WANNA TRY A GOOD CUP OF TAPU COCOA?
I'LL TREAT YOU TO ONE IF YOU MANAGE TO COME DOWN TO...
...TEAM SKULL'S BASE.
...
MAYBE PEOPLE LIKE YOU AND GUZMA ARE MORE SUITED TO BECOME THE KAHUNA...
...THAN SOMEONE LIKE ME WHO INSISTED THAT ALOLAN PROBLEMS SHOULD BE DEALT WITH BY ALOLAN PEOPLE.
WHAAAT?! BUT I BET HE'D SAY, "I DON'T WANT TO BECOME THE STUPID KAHUNA OF A STUPID ALOLAN ISLAND!"
HA HA HA...
WELL THEN, LET'S HEAD FOR MT. LANAKILA...
HUNH?

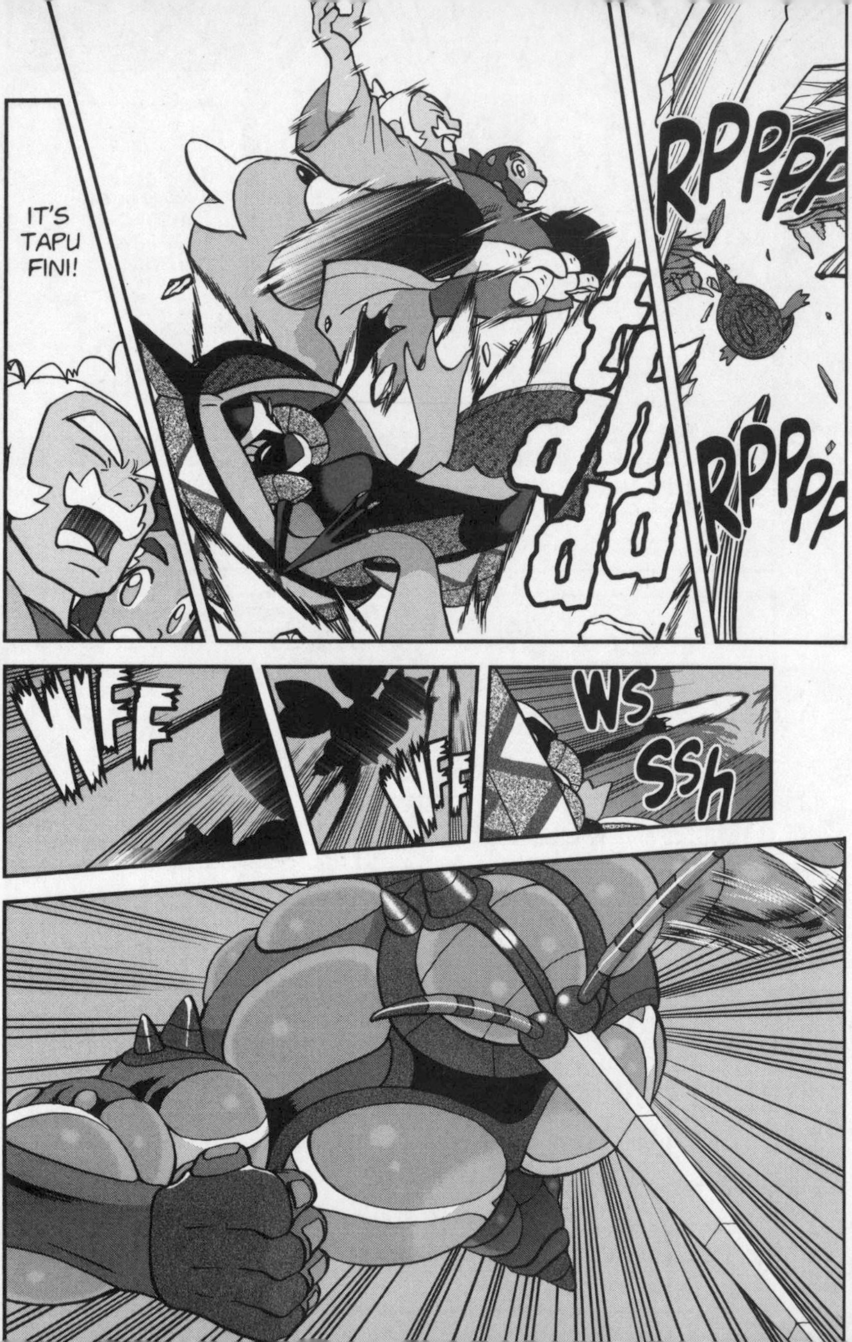
RPPPP
RPPPP
IT'S TAPU FINI!
WS
SSH
WFF
WFF

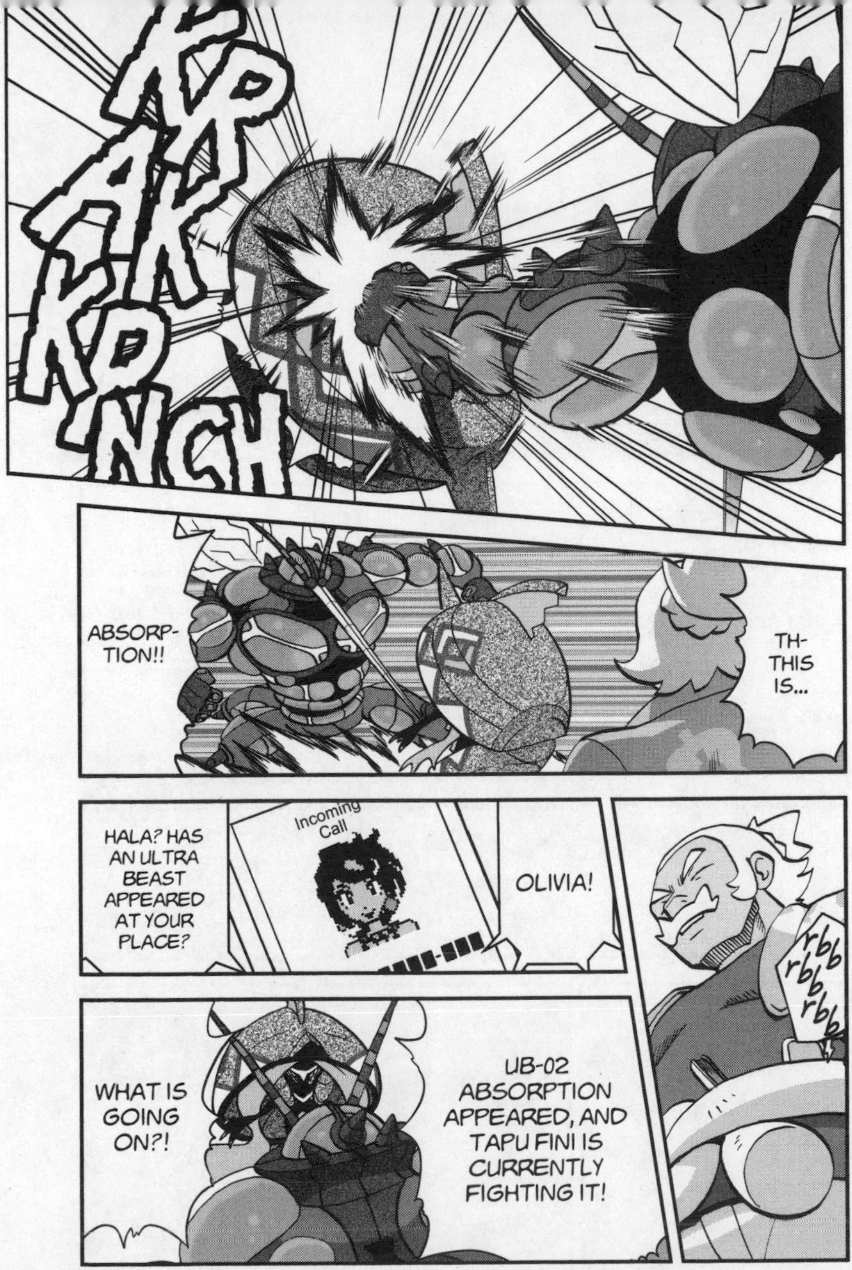
KRAKKRNCH
TH-THIS IS...
ABSORPTION!!
rbb rbb rbb
OLIVIA!
Incoming Call
HALA? HAS AN ULTRA BEAST APPEARED AT YOUR PLACE?
UB-02 ABSORPTION APPEARED, AND TAPU FINI IS CURRENTLY FIGHTING IT!
WHAT IS GOING ON?!

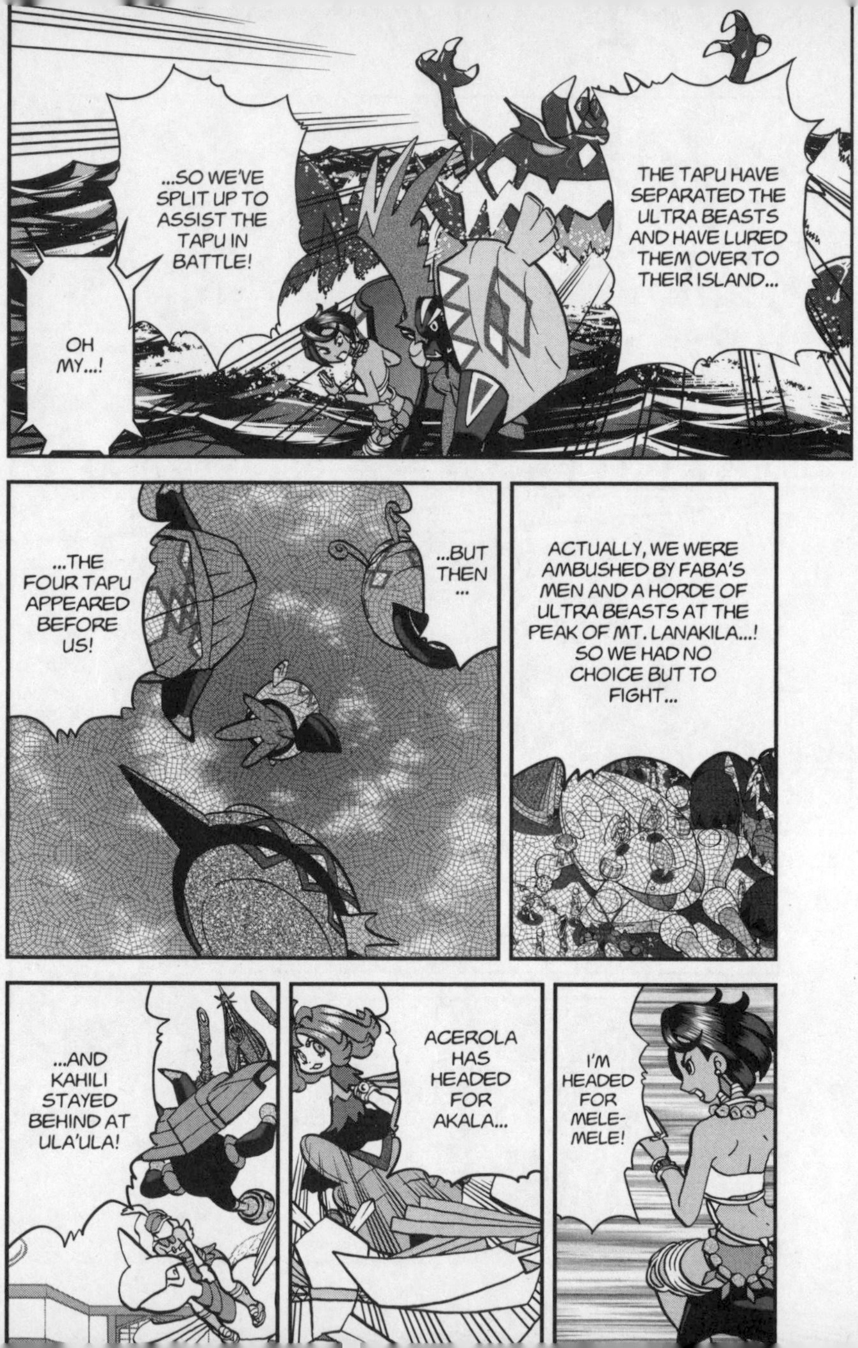
THE TAPU HAVE SEPARATED THE ULTRA BEASTS AND HAVE LURED THEM OVER TO THEIR ISLAND...
...SO WE'VE SPLIT UP TO ASSIST THE TAPU IN BATTLE!
OH MY...!
ACTUALLY, WE WERE AMBUSHED BY FABA'S MEN AND A HORDE OF ULTRA BEASTS AT THE PEAK OF MT. LANAKILA...! SO WE HAD NO CHOICE BUT TO FIGHT...
...BUT THEN ...
...THE FOUR TAPU APPEARED BEFORE US!
I'M HEADED FOR MELE-MELE!
ACEROLA HAS HEADED FOR AKALA...
...AND KAHILI STAYED BEHIND AT ULA'ULA!

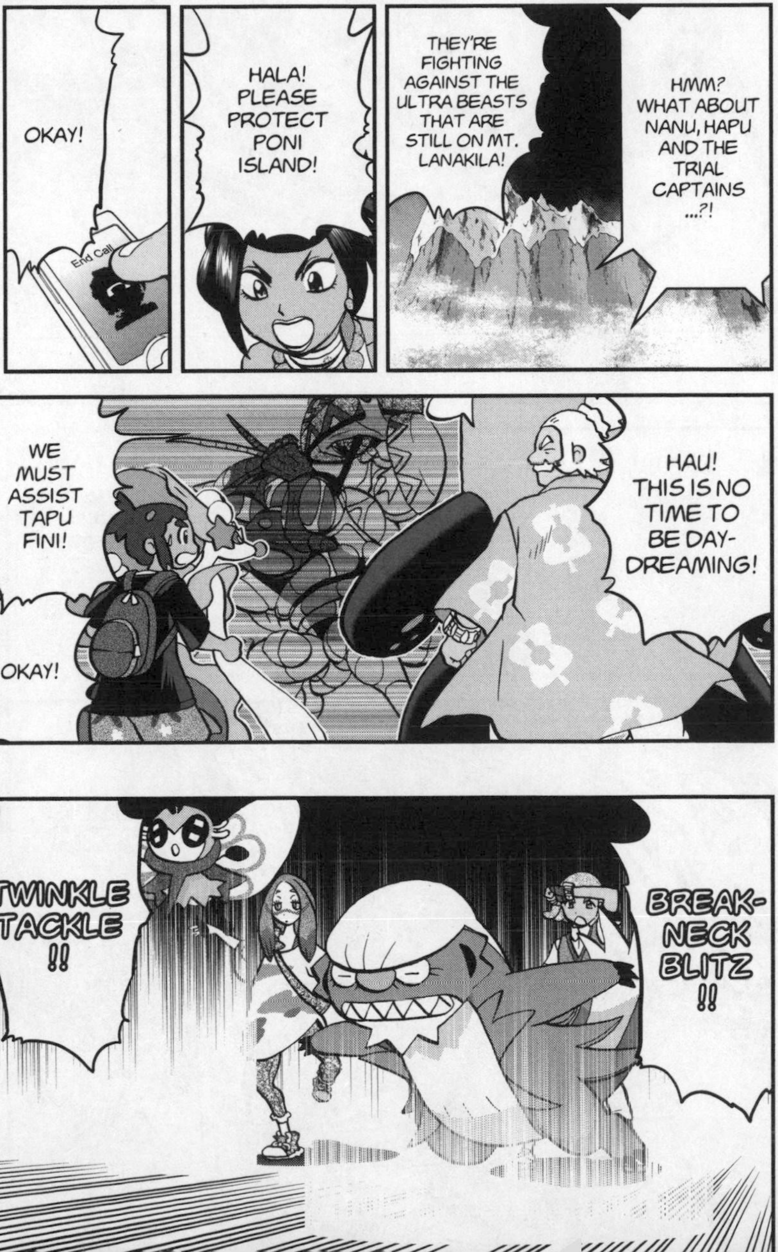
HMM? WHAT ABOUT NANU, HAPU AND THE TRIAL CAPTAINS ...?!
THEY'RE FIGHTING AGAINST THE ULTRA BEASTS THAT ARE STILL ON MT. LANAKILA!
HALA! PLEASE PROTECT PONI ISLAND!
End Call
OKAY!
HAU! THIS IS NO TIME TO BE DAY-DREAMING!
WE MUST ASSIST TAPU FINI!
OKAY!
BREAK-NECK BLITZ !!
TWINKLE TACKLE !!

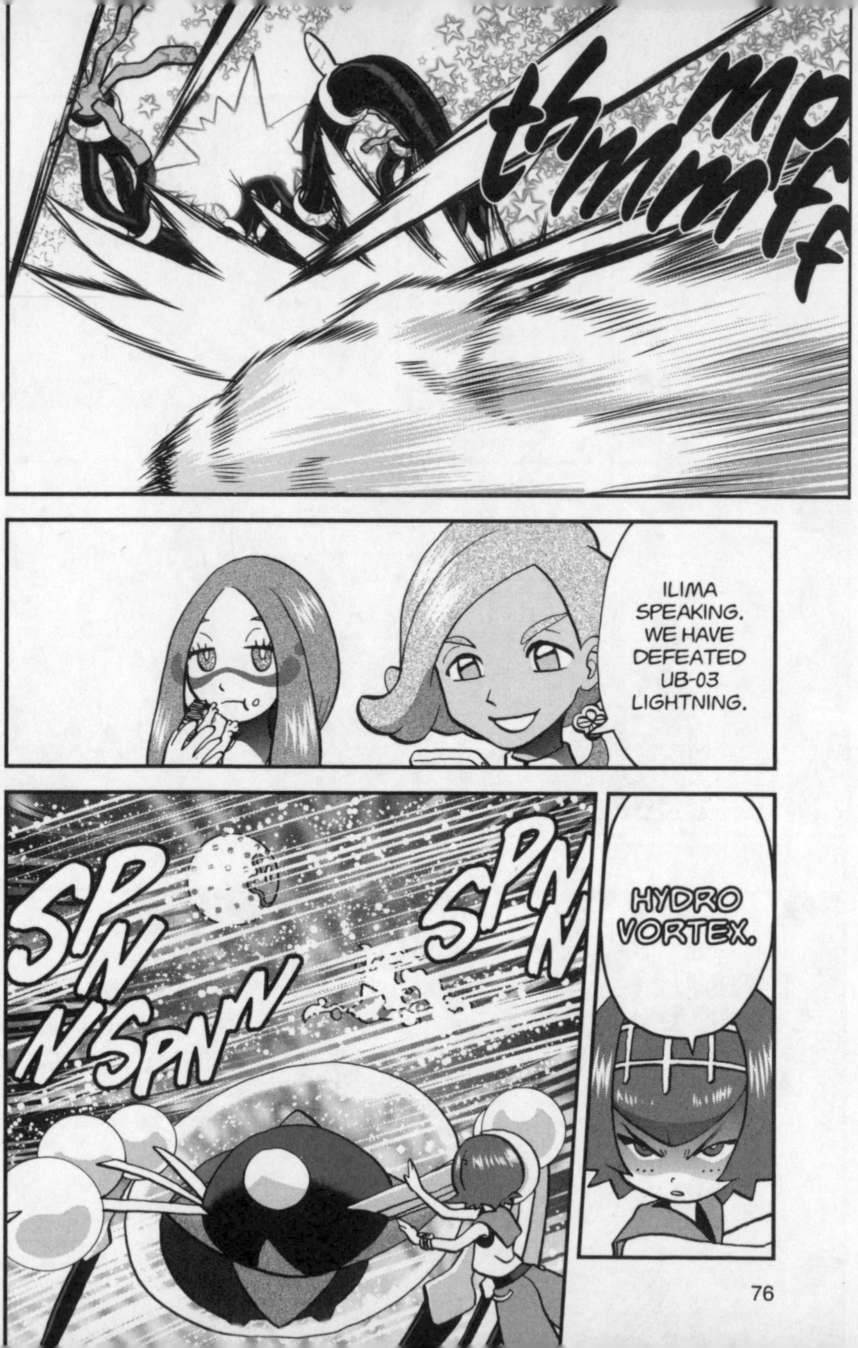
thmmp
thmmf
ILIMA SPEAKING. WE HAVE DEFEATED UB-03 LIGHTNING.
HYDRO VORTEX.
SPNN
SPNN
SPNN

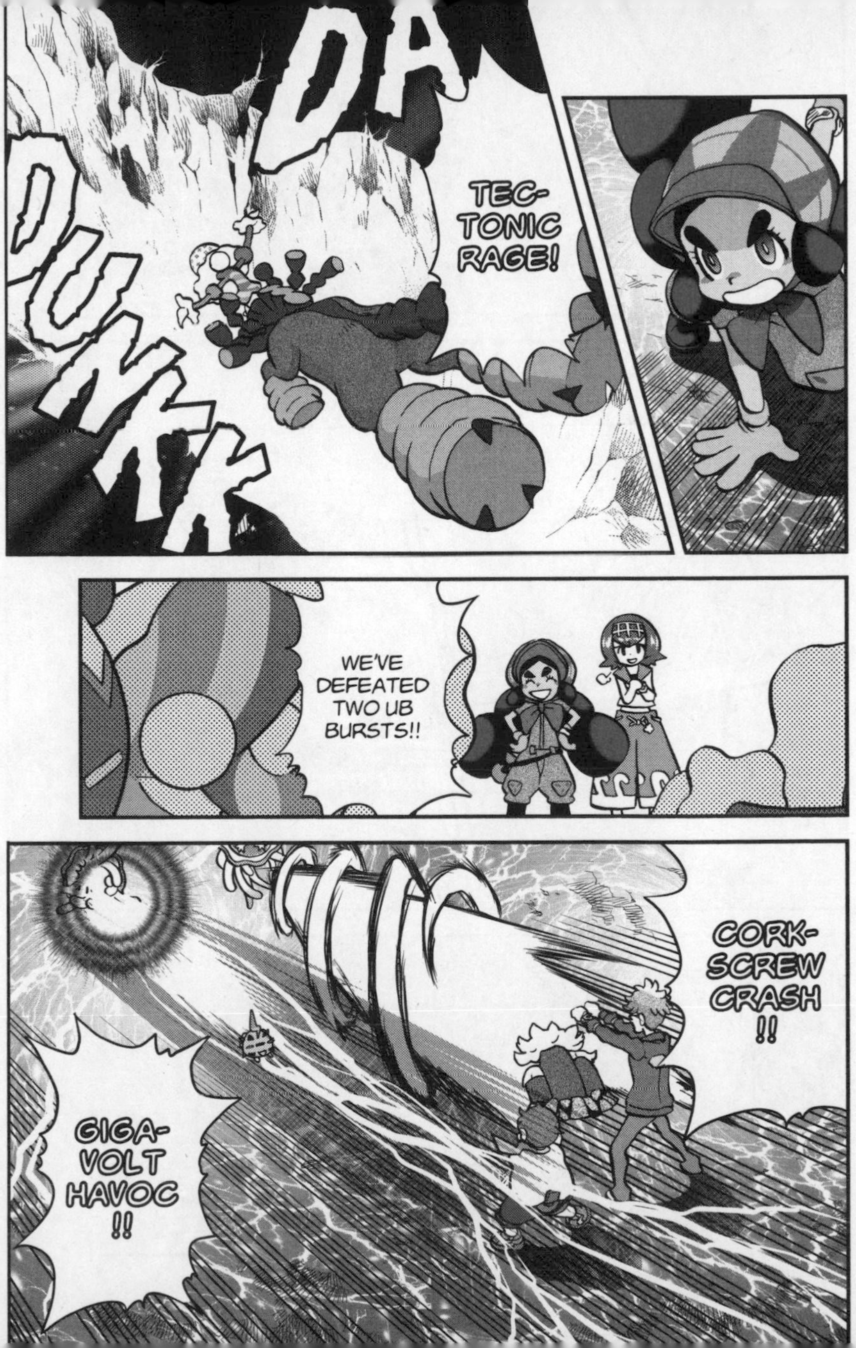
TEC-TONIC RAGE!
DA DUNKK
WE'VE DEFEATED TWO UB BURSTS!!
CORK-SCREW CRASH!!
GIGA-VOLT HAVOC!!

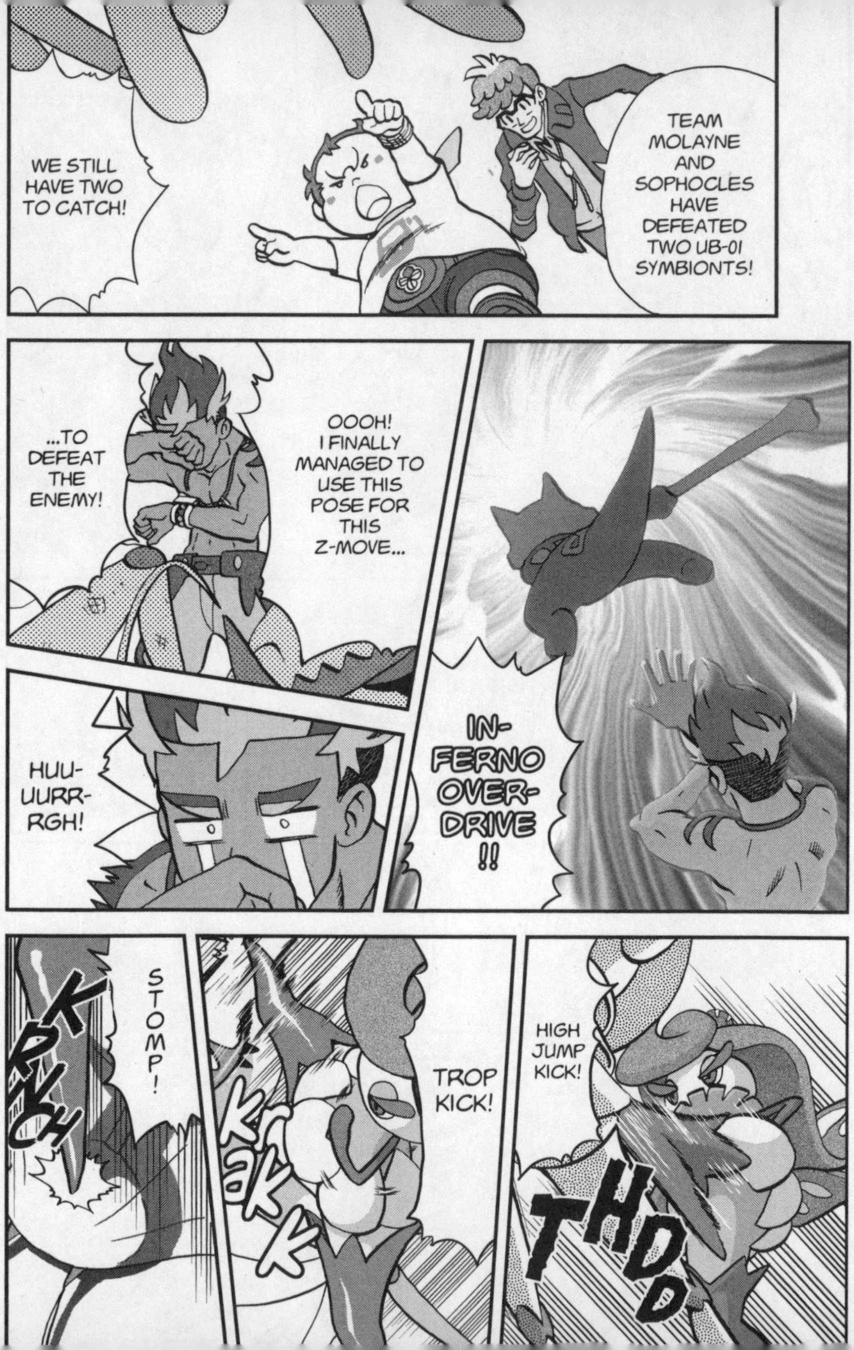
TEAM MOLAYNE AND SOPHOCLES HAVE DEFEATED TWO UB-01 SYMBIONTS!
WE STILL HAVE TWO TO CATCH!
IN-FERNO OVER-DRIVE !!
OOOH! I FINALLY MANAGED TO USE THIS POSE FOR THIS Z-MOVE...
...TO DEFEAT THE ENEMY!
HUU-UURR-RGH!
HIGH JUMP KICK!
THD
TROP KICK!
KKK
STOMP!
KRNCH

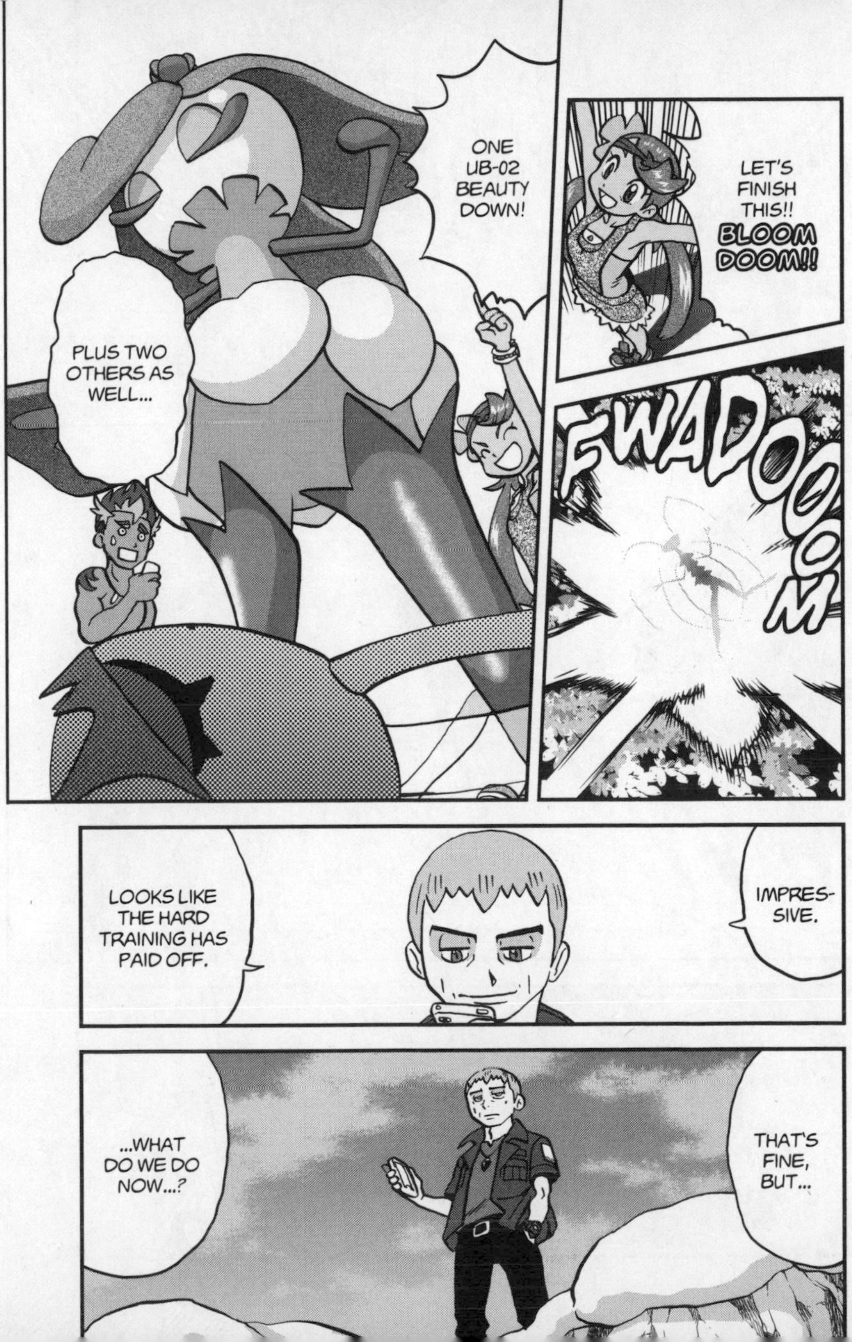
LET'S FINISH THIS!! BLOOM DOOM!!
FWADOOOOM
ONE UB-02 BEAUTY DOWN!
PLUS TWO OTHERS AS WELL...
IMPRES-SIVE.
LOOKS LIKE THE HARD TRAINING HAS PAID OFF.
THAT'S FINE, BUT...
...WHAT DO WE DO NOW...?

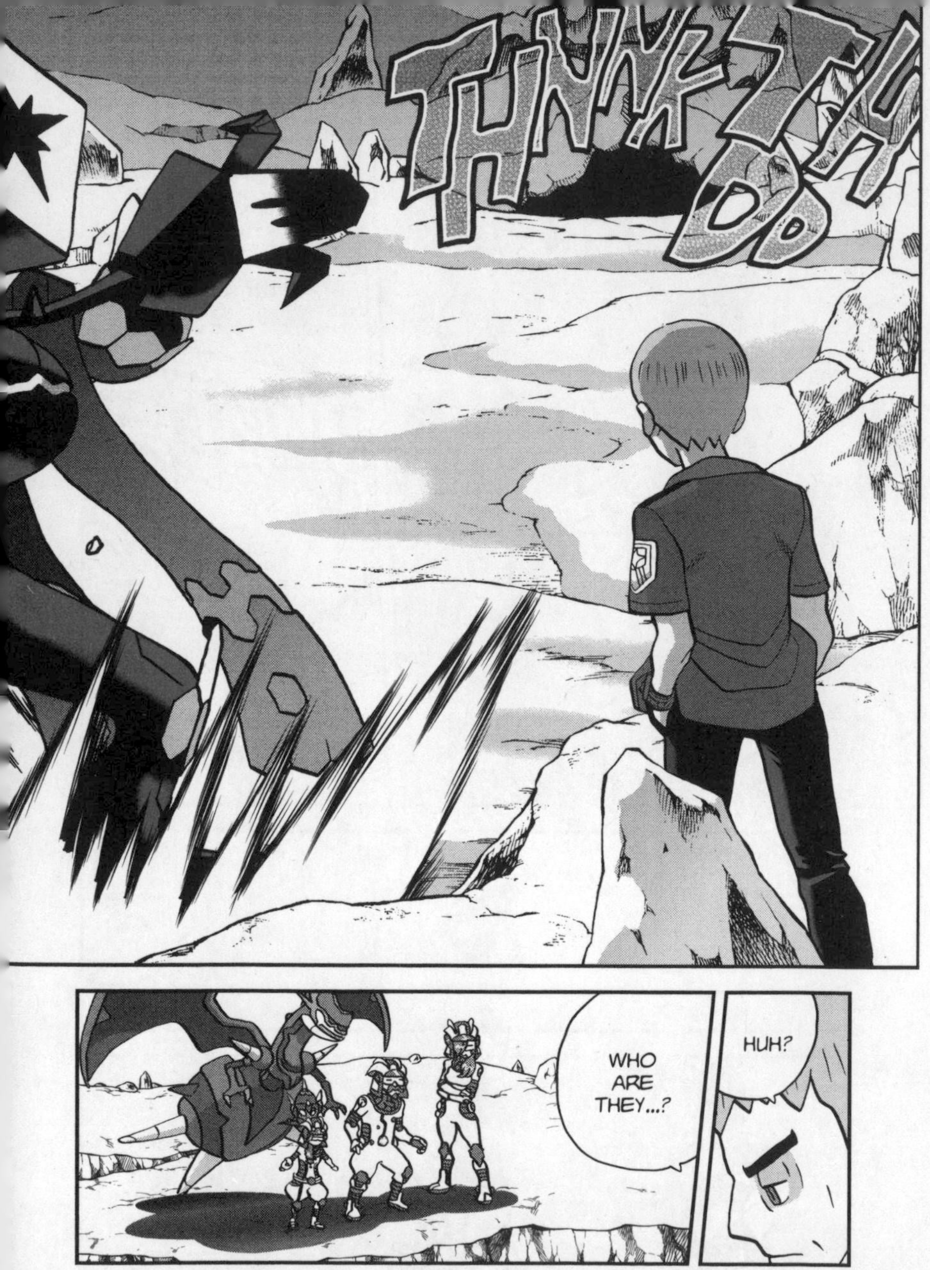
HUH?
WHO ARE THEY...?

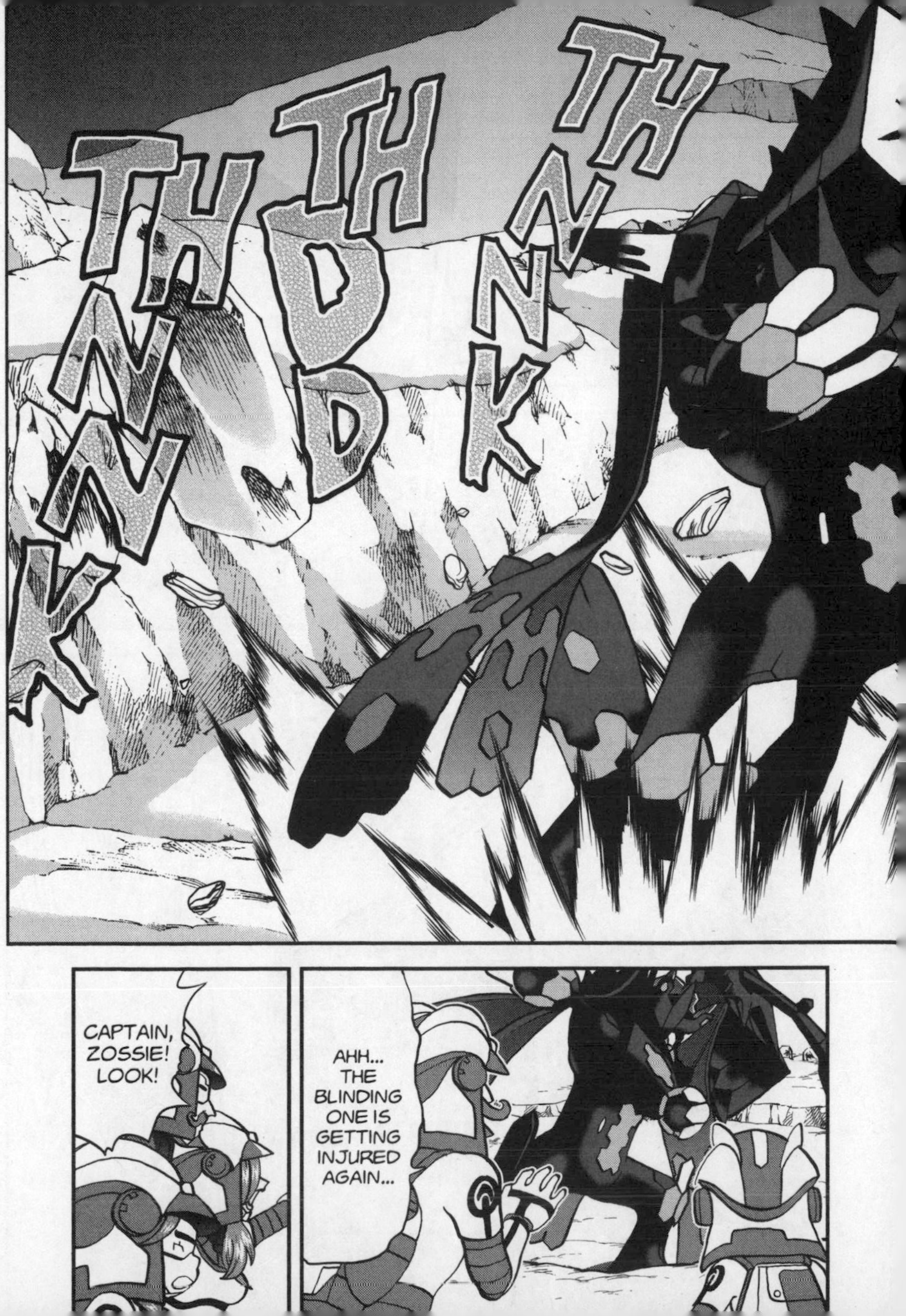
THNNK
THUDD
THNNNK
AHH... THE BLINDING ONE IS GETTING INJURED AGAIN...
CAPTAIN, ZOSSIE! LOOK!

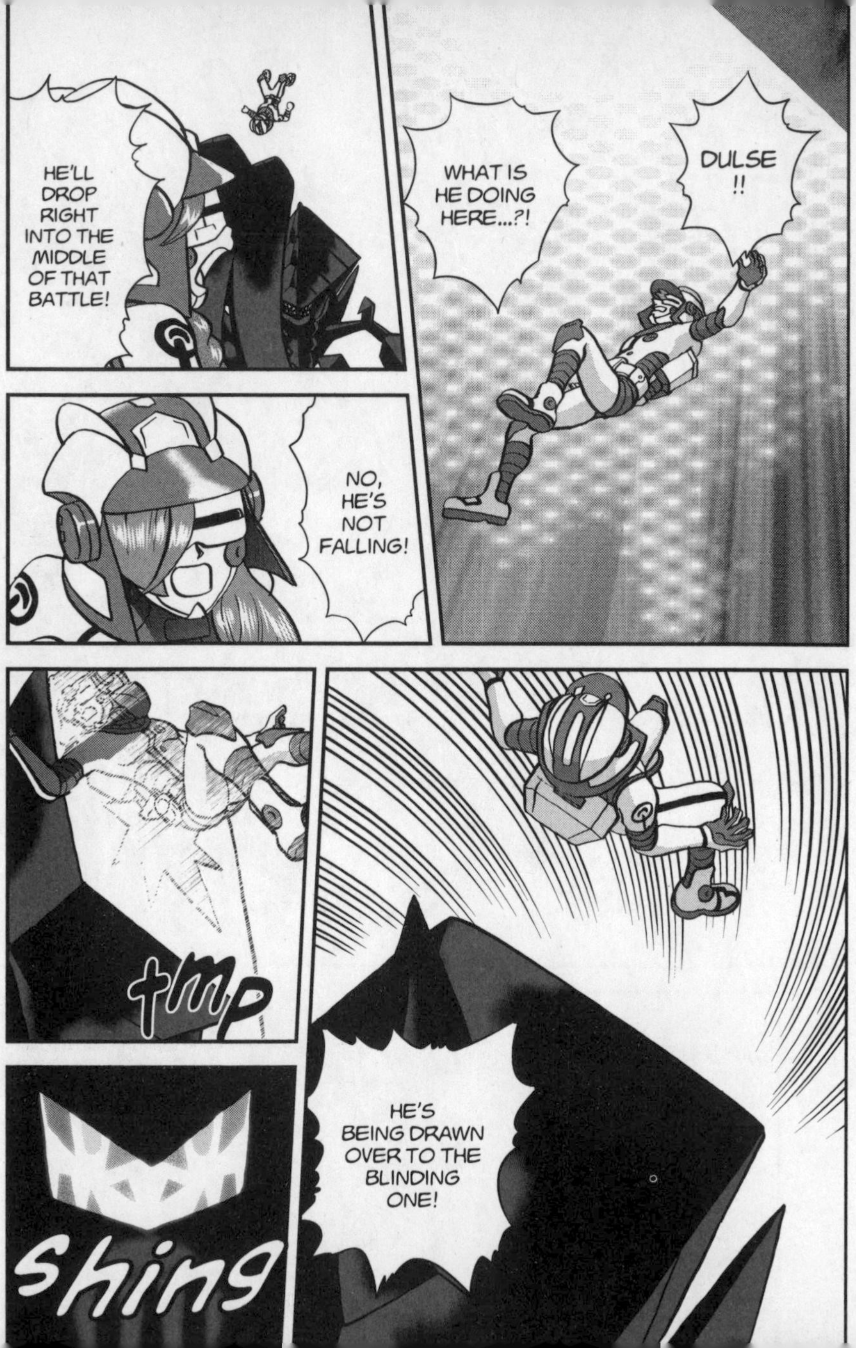
DULSE !!
WHAT IS HE DOING HERE...?!
HE'LL DROP RIGHT INTO THE MIDDLE OF THAT BATTLE!
NO, HE'S NOT FALLING!
HE'S BEING DRAWN OVER TO THE BLINDING ONE!
tmp
shing

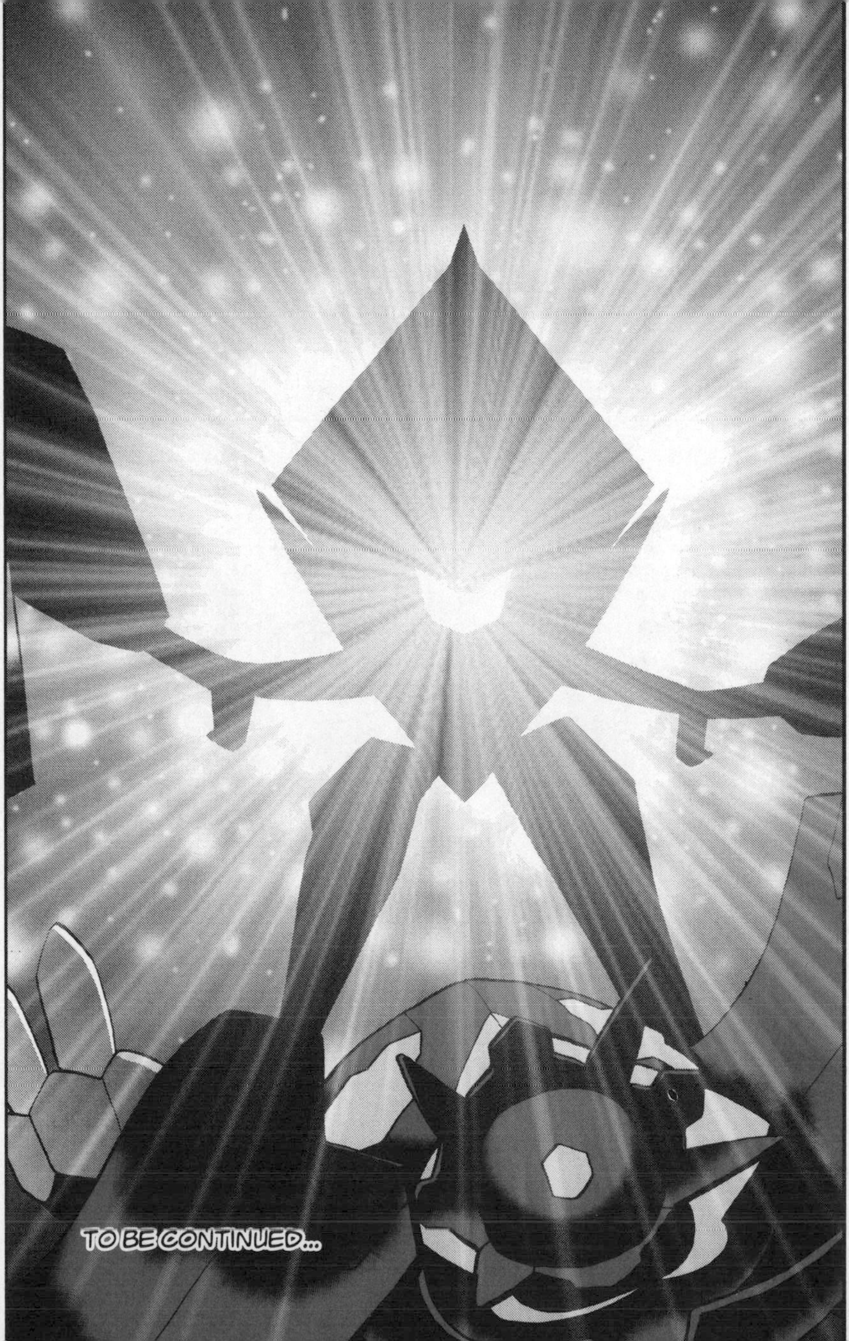
TO BE CONTINUED...

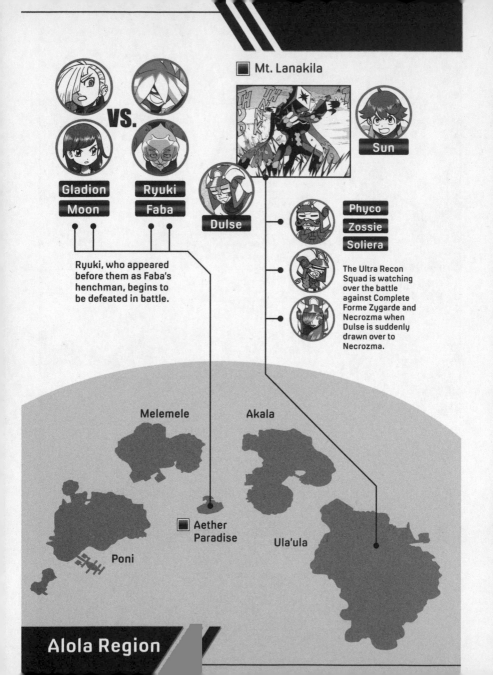

VS.

Gladion
Moon

Ryuki
Faba

Ryuki, who appeared before them as Faba's henchman, begins to be defeated in battle.

Mt. Lanakila

Sun

Dulse

Phyco
Zossie
Soliera

The Ultra Recon Squad is watching over the battle against Complete Forme Zygarde and Necrozma when Dulse is suddenly drawn over to Necrozma.

Melemele

Akala

Aether
Paradise

Ula'ula

Poni

Alola Region

Pokémon Sun & Moon
Volume 11
VIZ Media Edition

Story by HIDENORI KUSAKA
Art by SATOSHI YAMAMOTO

©2021 Pokémon.
©1995–2020 Nintendo / Creatures Inc. / GAME FREAK inc.
TM, ®, and character names are trademarks of Nintendo.
POCKET MONSTERS SPECIAL SUN • MOON Vol. 6
by Hidenori KUSAKA, Satoshi YAMAMOTO
© 2017 Hidenori KUSAKA, Satoshi YAMAMOTO
All rights reserved.
Original Japanese edition published by SHOGAKUKAN.
English translation rights in the United States of America, Canada, the United Kingdom,
Ireland, Australia and New Zealand arranged with SHOGAKUKAN.

Original Cover Design—Hiroyuki KAWASOME (grafio)

Translation—Tetsuichiro Miyaki
English Adaptation—Bryant Turnage
Touch-Up & Lettering—Susan Daigle-Leach
Design—Alice Lewis
Editor—Joel Enos

Printed in the U.S.A.

Published by
VIZ Media, LLC
P.O. Box 77010
San Francisco, CA 94107

10 9 8 7 6 5 4 3 2 1
First printing, September 2021

viz.com

Coming Next Volume

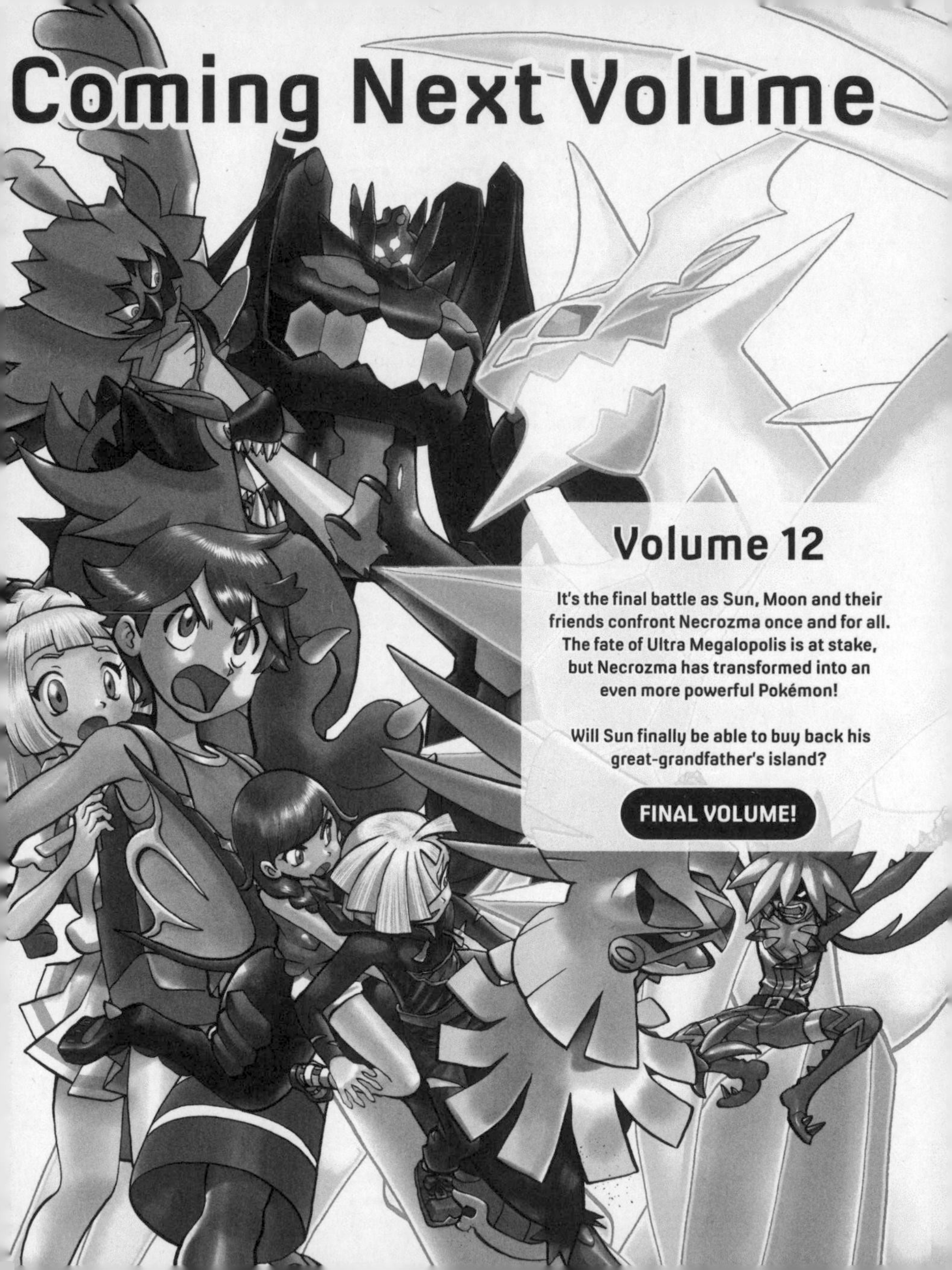

Volume 12

It's the final battle as Sun, Moon and their friends confront Necrozma once and for all. The fate of Ultra Megalopolis is at stake, but Necrozma has transformed into an even more powerful Pokémon!

Will Sun finally be able to buy back his great-grandfather's island?

FINAL VOLUME!

Pokémon

ADVENTURES

COLLECTOR'S EDITION

Story by **HIDENORI KUSAKA**   Art by **MATO**

A stylish new omnibus edition of the best-selling *Pokémon Adventures* manga, collecting all the original volumes of the series you know and love!

ALL YOUR FAVORITE *POKÉMON* GAME CHARACTERS JUMP OUT OF THE SCREEN INTO THE PAGES OF THIS ACTION-PACKED MANGA!

THIS IS THE END OF THIS GRAPHIC NOVEL!

To properly enjoy this VIZ Media graphic novel, please turn it around and begin reading from right to left.

This book has been printed in the original Japanese format in order to preserve the orientation of the original artwork. Have fun with it!

READ THIS WAY!

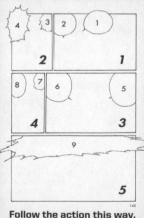

Follow the action this way.